Award Nominations

Shortlisted for the Saboteur Award: Best Novella 2019

Shortlisted for the Saltire Society First Book Award 2018

Shortlisted for Manchester Metropolitan University/
Liverpool John Moores University: Novella Award 2016

Book of the Month

DIVA Magazine - September 2018

Scottish Review of Books - November 2018.

Praise for Amphibian

"Amphibian is a strange aquatic joy, sodden with the mischief-making of contemporary satire. Through gleeful transformation of reality into the surreal, where rising water levels and bobbing molluscs have competition from coworkers for oddest office feature, Neuwirth establishes herself as a writer with a talent for spearing the absurdity of everyday life. Eat it up in shark-size bites."
-Laura Waddell

"Amphibian is a wryly poignant parable, surreal and tender, with a wit drier than…well, you'll see. Sweetly realised details give teasing life to a story of daily routine, self-doubt, small rebellions, and sometimes just missing the bigger picture."
-Rachel McCrum

"It often takes a fantasy to accurately describe reality, and this screwy little fable cuts sharply into contemporary life. With wit and heart, Amphibian reveals the messiness, absurdity and terror beneath the apparent banalities of the workplace as only a good story can, with characters as real as their situation is impossible."
-Harry Josephine Giles

"I urge you to read Amphibian: a little book with a big message, full of whip-smart writing. I can't wait to read more from Christina Neuwirth."
-Claire Askew

"Amphibian finds much humour in the sheer tedium and pointlessness of modern-day office work. At times the novella felt like entering the miniature world of a snow globe and being tipped upside down. Neuwirth is an exciting and endearing new voice."
-Shane Strachan

"What a smart story Amphibian is, packed full of sly observations on the hazards, joys and accommodations required of modern office life. Written with an engaging deadpan style that belies its fantastical premise, this neat and watery confection is wryly humorous, but with a dark little heart."
-Mary Paulson-Ellis

"Amphibian takes a simple but inventive premise and pushes it to brilliant and ridiculous lengths. The writing is deft and playful, full of wonderful jokes and observations, and a carefully-drawn cast of characters. The book brims with undisguised joy and a wonderful humanity. It is a story of tricky, boring, mundane reality prismed through a delightful fantasy."
-Ross McCleary

A perfect novella. Short, sharp and weird and shimmery.
–Helen McClory

***

"Neuwirth's debut is an unsettling novella where Gwendoline Riley's uncomfortable close up on realism meets Kirsty Logan's aquatic take on magic realism, when management at Rose Ellis's office make a decision to close her department that gives new meaning to the phrase 'going under'. As the office gradually begins to fill with water as an incentive to productivity, Rose flips half heartedly between rebellion and a pragmatic adaptation in a biting satire of office life mixed with dreamy sensuality and a wry, anti-capitalist undertone about the corrosive effects of austerity."
-Kaite Welsh, DIVA Magazine

"Wonderfully weird, witty and heart-felt — anyone who has ever so much as stepped foot in an office will fall in love with this."
–Chiara Bullen, CommonSpace

Amphibian

Christina Neuwirth

Speculative Books

The right of Christina Neuwirth to be identified as
the author of this work has been asserted by her in
accordance with the Copyright, Design and Patents Act,
1988

First published in 2018 by Speculative Books Ltd
speculativebooks.net
@spec_books

A CIP catalogue record for this book is available from
the British Library
ISBN - 978-1-9999180-9-5

Cover design by Anna Toffolo
www.annatoffolo.co.uk
Chapter Numbers - Moonshake Design
@MoonshakeDesign
Edited by Jennifer Hutchison
@Jenn1H
Typesetting by Dale McMullen
@DalePMcMullen

This is a work of fiction. Any similarity between
the characters and situations within its pages and
places or persons, living or dead, is unintentional and
coincidental.

3 5 7 9 8 6 4

For my mum.

From: lmerc@moneytowncashgrowth.co.uk
To: All Staff
CC: ehump@moneytowncashgrowth.co.uk
Subject: 1st Quarter Sales Review

Dear Colleague,

I am writing to inform you that, after the last Sales Review, the revenues from the fourth floor have been deemed less than satisfactory. It has therefore been decided that the fourth floor will be gradually put under water, effective tomorrow morning, 26 June.

This is a decision passed on from our CEO and is entirely outside of my control.

The measure will take effect until further notice. If sales pick up over the course of the next quarter, the flood will be reviewed and submitted for potential reversal.

Should you have any questions about this, please direct these to the CEO's assistant, Mr Evan Humperdink.

Many thanks,

Lynn Mercer,
Regional Sales Division Director

MoneyTownCashGrowth
Bonds | Promises | Trust

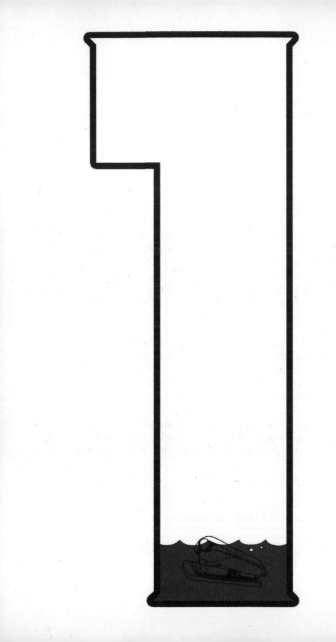

TUESDAY

Rose was late for work. She was speed-walking across the Meadows, barely looking up from her phone to swerve and avoid dog walkers and cyclists. A true genius at multi-tasking, she scrolled through her work group email at the same time. Yeah, yeah, corporate whatever. She saw another notification pop up on her phone's screen. She smiled to herself: her cousin liked her Instagram picture of the sky; her day was off to a good start.

She entered the cool lobby of Tollcross Mansion, a misleadingly named block of glass and metal in the middle of an ancient church yard. Rose enjoyed the view, but the building itself made her feel uneasy and on display. She thought she might fry if the direct sunlight, amplified by the big windows, lasted for too long. At least they gave her something to look out of while she sold Bonds and Promises to fancy, important clients.

Rose loved her job. No, that's a lie. But she tolerated it, as well as you could expect her to. After all, she was only there until she found something better. She had only been there until she found something better for the past six years.

Wave to the girl at the desk. Hi, girl at desk! Rose straightened her jacket and felt for the waistband of her trousers to make sure they weren't sliding down. Walk to the lift while humming hellos at other colleagues. Push the button. Was the girl looking at her differently today? Was there pity in her eyes? Itchy contacts? Probably just an eyelash, thought Rose. Get in the lift. Press 4. She walked to the back, to the mirror, but avoided her own eyes and made room for everyone else to get on. They pushed buttons for the upper floors, mostly. Management. She was just a sales peg, creating income, while the others on her lift were thinking heads with shiny iMacs.

Rose was the first to get off the lift. She smelled something musty wafting towards her. Her foot sank into the carpet. Water bubbled around it. She thought of quicksand. Shit! Her brogues! They were new and made Rose feel like a 1920s gentleman, which, paired with the low-rising pinstripe trousers and her pinned-up hair, created the androgynous look she hoped made her appear assertive, cool and a bit dangerous. The shoes were fucked now. Soaked. She had sunk half an inch deep into the purple carpet, which was sopping wet.

Rose looked around the reception area. She squished across the hallway, and Trevor looked up, nodding a greeting.

'Hiya, Rose. How are you?'

'Good, good. What about you?' she said. Trevor nodded and made some affirmative noises. He was good. Trevor was always good. He was a nice amount of chatty. He had a bit of a distracted look about him, and his wispy ginger hair stuck up around his head like he was about to float away on the slightest breeze. Rose assumed he had a very involving game of Solitaire going on. She slumped onwards across the marshy carpet. Down the corridor, small ripples were being stirred up by the heels of the woman walking towards her. She looked up from her clipboard and smiled without saying anything, little Rhian with her perfect drawn-on eyebrows.

At the end of the corridor, finally, Room 4.02, her office. Well, it would be an exaggeration to say 4.02 was *her* office; Rose did share it with Siobhan, but she was often away in the field, selling Promises directly to her customers. Even the thought of Siobhan's job made Rose's skin crawl – selling Bonds and Promises on the phone was bad enough, and she couldn't bear the notion of actually going to people's houses and bothering them in their personal space. Alas, Siobhan was here today, sitting on her swivel chair.

There was a golden labrador perched on her lap.

'Hi, Rose!' Siobhan said.

Rose felt her face grow hot and, she was sure, red. After months of barely seeing Siobhan, of looking only at her desk and wondering about the person who had chosen to arrange their pens by size, she was finally here. Their induction periods had overlapped but she hadn't really spent any time with her. Siobhan was very tall and very beautiful and seemed to Rose to have her life entirely in order. With every growing second in her presence she felt herself fall apart more and more, her hair escaping its clips, her clothes accumulating wrinkles. She tried not to look directly at Siobhan, in case her radiance burnt the retinas off her eyes.

'Hiya. Um,' but before Rose could formulate a coherent question, or something resembling it, Siobhan had already released a flood of explanations.

'Well, Sterlington is really scared of the water, you see, and when we came in it was all like this, I mean I'd read the email, obviously, but I didn't know how bad it would be. So I called upstairs and they said that it's just going to be like this, but it's nothing to worry about, really. But Sterlington's really quite frightened of water so he's sitting here for now until I can get an armchair moved up from the third floor,' she said, patting the large dog on the head, which was level with her own.

Sterlington looked heavy, but Siobhan's face didn't betray any signs of strain.

That's what love looks like, Rose thought.

Rose wondered whether the water would be dripping from the ceiling onto the third floor slackers from 'marketing', doing their font changes on Photoshop and then taking a fifty-minute coffee break. She sometimes went down there to use the scanners. Time always appeared to move at a different pace, less frantic, more deliberate. Their daily goals must be very different from the sales department, if Rose's to-do list was anything to go by.

Siobhan bent her body around Sterlington to reach her computer's keyboard, and furiously typed some words.

'They said they'll be here soon. You don't mind, right? A little chair for the office? It'll be nice.'

Rose didn't mind getting a new chair, but she did wonder why Siobhan was back from her assignments and cramping her office's solo style. She shrugged her shoulders in what she hoped was a passable imitation of friendly agreement or non-threatening indifference. Then she walked over to her desk, stepped out of her still wet brogues, and sat down on her chair, dragging her feet back and forth through the puddle underneath.

Scanning the wall by the windows, Rose spotted a six-socket multi-plug sitting in the inch of water lapping at its greying sides. A flash of a health and safety video from primary school appeared in Rose's head, a video of a hairdryer falling into a bathtub, but she was already standing in the water, and so was Siobhan, and yet somehow they were fine. The electricity was still working and nobody was being fried alive.

Not boiling to death in an electric soup – that was the upside.

Siobhan saw her looking at the plugs. She must've also seen the concern in her eyes because she said, 'Oh, don't worry about the plugs. They had the cablers in this morning. We're fine.'

'Sure,' said Rose. The cablers.

Siobhan nodded. Her eyes glazed over again as she kept grooming the dog on her lap, reading something on her screen.

'So,' said Rose.

Siobhan peeked out from behind the dog's head.

'Yeah?'

'This water thing.'

'Yeah, it's annoying, isn't it?'

'Pretty annoying. What did you do about your shoes?'

'Waterproof. I came prepared,' Siobhan said and stuck out a shiny ankle boot. Rose rolled her chair to the edge of her desk to see.

'Cute.'

The rolling chair made ripples and water splashed up against the two desks.

Sterlington flinched and let out a sad little warble.

'It's not so bad. What did you go for?' asked Siobhan.

'Took them off. Now I've got wet socks,' said Rose.

'Just take your socks off! I don't mind.'

As if to show his agreement, Sterlington licked at the side of Siobhan's computer screen.

Rose shuddered in disgust. Show her toes? They were so long and monkey-like, good for holding onto a surfboard, but not for anyone else to see. Oh well, maybe the water would go away tomorrow and she'd only have to walk around in wet socks for a day.

A knock on the door interrupted this very important train of thought.

'Oh, hey, Robert.'

Tall, broad-shouldered and made entirely of bones, Robert from Room 4.37 two doors down appeared in the doorway.

'We're seeing if we can create a current so we can float memos along to the big room. Want to come?'

'No, we're okay,' said Siobhan.

'Excuse me,' said a man in a pigeon blue cardigan, carrying a floral armchair. He squeezed past Robert and placed the armchair in the corner of the office, where a potted fern had died a few months ago. Rose had never wanted to throw it out because she still held on to the naïve hope that it might come back to life one day. Maybe now that its roots were submerged in water, it would have a fighting chance.

Siobhan got up, carried Sterlington to the chair, sat him down, and brushed his long blonde hairs from her black high-waisted trousers. They were made from that annoying fabric that, if worn by anyone who wasn't Siobhan, had a tendency to attract dust bunnies, hair and definitely yoghurt stains. Rose had never bought anything made from that fabric because she attracted these items onto her clothes anyway.

Rose wanted to see how the rest of the floor was dealing with the water situation. She followed Robert to 4.37, a room filled with ten desks and ten computers and lots of screens, because multiple screens make you more efficient, or whatever. She didn't understand how having more screens would make you sell more bonds and promises to people, but maybe that was because she wasn't very interested in selling them in the first place.

There was a desk fan standing on the floor next to Robert's desk – the cablers had been, Rose reminded herself, the water is fine. The fan was switched on to high, and created a ripple in the inch of water that covered the floor. A little paper boat sailed proudly from Robert's desk to Kerry's, who was making a flag for the ship from a book of stamps, purple lip gloss and a cocktail stick. Rose folded a boat of her own and crouched down to blow wind into its sail, which was made from a tissue taped to more cocktail sticks. After a good twenty minutes of racing, Robert's boat won a trophy he had made himself out of shiny gum wrappers. Rose suspected foul play. Before she had a chance to appeal, a distinct splashing and clacking interrupted the prize-giving ceremony.

Lynn Mercer had been Head of the Sales Division for two years and Rose knew that she felt like she was the only capable person in the place. Her hair was in a high bun that looked like it never came undone, not even when she slept or took a shower. Rose looked at Lynn's feet and saw that she was in heels, the water slapping around her toes.

Click. Another step.

Splash.

'What's this?'

'Just testing,' said Robert.

'The water,' offered Kerry, helpfully.

'Yes. Well. It's exactly that sort of behaviour that got us all into this pickle in the first place, isn't it?' said Lynn.

Lynn liked to ask questions.

Lynn also liked to use words like 'pickle'.

'Well?'

The room was quiet. The desk fan was still sending ripples from Robert's desk at the front all the way to where Rhian was sitting, right at the back, by the window. A small paper boat sailed by.

'*This* has happened,' Lynn swept a hand around the general floor area and hesitated for a second.

Rose hoped she might not carry on and leave it at this philosophical statement. But no, there was more.

'... because our sales have been very bad. Kerry, what have our figures been, roughly?'

'Two- um, two-hundred,' said Kerry and fiddled with the lid of the purple lip gloss.

'Two-hundred what?'

'Sales.'

Instead of hissing more words, Lynn was now squinting

so hard at Kerry that Rose thought her eyebrows might merge in the middle.

'Per week.'

A gasp resounded around the big office.

'Are you sure that's right?' Robert had now turned around to look at Kerry. She looked down at the keyboard, clicked her mouse and looked back at the screen.

'Yup.'

'Jesus.'

'And this is exactly why we're going under,' said Lynn.

She liked a good exit line, so at this point she turned around, ready to march down the hallway and past reception to her secluded corner office. 'Corner office' makes it sound fancier than it was, because corner offices conjure up thoughts of New York and shiny buildings and great views. Lynn's corner office was just an office in a corner, with two windows and a fish tank.

But she didn't get to leave just yet. Siobhan, who had walked down the hallway to see what was going on, entered Room 4.37. As if the new arrival had freed them from Lynn's spell, the others in the room started asking questions like: 'What the hell? Since when was it okay to just flood an office? Couldn't they have told them sooner? They'd call the union reps – this was atrocious; and besides, the printer in the hallway is still broken, when is that ever going to get fixed, and how were they meant to be selling Bonds and Promises when they couldn't even print them out and send them properly, anyway?'

Lynn was overwhelmed. She waved her hand around again, as if to divert the crowd's attention through excessive movement. It worked, and everyone got a little distracted. 'Look, don't start with me. Take it up with Evan on the seventh floor. Read the bloody email! This is all above my pay grade. I never decided any of this.' Drowned out by more questions, she added – and Rose heard – 'Nobody asked me.'

Rose might have felt something like pity for Lynn, but it was quickly replaced by annoyance, and the need to tuck in the laundry tag that was sticking out of the back of Kerry's blouse.

'When will it go away?' Rose asked, stepping closer to Lynn. The flurry of questions quietened down.

'I can't say. This is a disciplinary measure. It could be permanent,' Rose drew in a sharp breath while Lynn spoke, 'but, but it probably isn't. Look, we just need to pick up the pace. Get the synergy going.' The last bit she said with her voice raised, because the others in the big office had started protesting.

Robert stepped up next to Rose and she saw a vein on his neck pop out. He might be about to swear at Lynn. Was he about to swear at Lynn? Rose put her hand on his arm. The vein receded.

'And you don't have any more information on it?'

'I'm afraid I don't, Robert, and I resent that tone,' she shook her head a little, but her bun stayed rigid. Despite herself, Rose had to admit she was impressed by its structural integrity.

Finally, Siobhan pulled Rose away by her elbow and led her into their office. Her fingers were firm and gentle on the thin fabric of Rose's blazer. When they got back, Sterlington was still sitting on the armchair, curled up and yellow, his fur only wet at the ends. He looked very comfortable there and appeared to be sleeping.

When Siobhan kicked the door shut behind her it made a wave.

'So that was useless,' she said.

'Maybe you didn't hear all of it,' said Rose tentatively. She hadn't thought of Siobhan as the door-kicking kind.

'No, I heard it. I heard when she said nothing!' Siobhan kept talking as Rose walked over to her own desk about how they should write to Mr Humperdink, and this was a disgrace, and how could their own management not know what was going on? Rose thought they probably wouldn't be able to make any difference anyway, not without working their way slowly up the tangle of bureaucracy.

But Siobhan was unstoppable. A righteous rage was in her eyes and in the tips of her hair like static. She sat down – ripples from her swivel chair rocking against Rose's feet – and began furiously typing what Rose assumed was a draft complaint email. Rose shrugged, and dipped her toe back into the water.

Wet socks.

Fuck.

With a sigh, Rose waded over to Siobhan's desk to peer over her shoulder.

```
From: smurp@moneytowncashgrowth.co.uk
To: ehump@moneytowncashgrowth.co.uk
Subject: RE: Flooding

Dear Mr Humperdink,

What the actual fuck? This is
unacceptable.
```

How can we make this go away?

Best wishes, Siobhan (from the fourth floor. Where the water is up to my ankles, by the way)

Rose laughed. She very much longed to lean over Siobhan's shoulder, grab the mouse and press send. But she didn't. Siobhan didn't turn around, just leaned back in her seat to give Rose a clear view of the message on the screen.

Even the unsent message made Rose nervous. She knew that sometimes programmes saved messages you never end up sending, so she cleared all her caches and histories regularly, mostly so that Google searches for a new job wouldn't show up in her performance evaluation.

Lately she'd been looking at jobs on boats. The thought of not having to go to the office every day seemed so appealing, and you'd technically *live* in your office, so you'd never be late to work. Instead of having to buy an increasing number of slightly varied types of blouses, you could get away with wearing the same thing every day, and all of it looked comfy, in a rugged way: waxy yellow coats, big jumpers, wellies, thick socks. There probably wouldn't be any internet on the boat either, so she wouldn't have to answer any emails. As a skipper, she'd never have to make a sales call again. She set a reminder on her phone to look up what a skipper actually did.

Rose walked back to her desk, her every step squelching on the carpet. Siobhan moved on to a different task after deleting and double-deleting the harsh draft. It was kind of nice, Rose thought, having someone else there with her, although it did mean she couldn't listen to her music without headphones. Rose made a start on her own email to management. Got to be polite, now. Politeness never fails.

From: relli@moneytowncashgrowth.co.uk
To: ehump@moneytowncashgrowth.co.uk
Subject: Flooding

Dear Mr Humperdink,

Concerning the flooding, it seems to be the case that—
Concerning the flooding, it has come to my recent attention that-
It has come to my recent-
I am sure it has come to your attention-

As I am certain you're aware, the entire fourth floor seems to be slightly flooded. As this doesn't appear to influence the electrical equipment, the only inconvenient occurrence is the dampness of my colleagues' and my own footwear. If we could please get your input on how to remedy this situation, that would be much appreciated.

Also, what the actual fuck?
Best wishes,
Rose (damp-socked)

She did some more editing before printing a test copy. A test copy was definitely necessary. But because the

printer in the hallway was still broken she had to send
it to the printer at reception and collect it from Trevor.
She showed the print-out to Siobhan, who laughed at the
actual fuck, took out some of the snarkiness and inserted
more perhapses and perchances, before turning her
attention to beating her own Minesweeper high score.
Rose was surprised by how good Siobhan was at it.

'You can't possibly be too polite, you know,' Siobhan
said and defused ten bombs. The glint in her eye was
electric.

Rose agreed, if somewhat reluctantly. Evan was, after
all, the man who was probably sitting by the tap turning
the water on and off at will, you wouldn't want to screw
that up.

Evan Humperdink wasn't even their boss. He was the
CEO's assistant, which, Rose assumed, made him feel a)
entitled, b) slightly underpaid and c) power-mad every
time he actually got put in charge of a project. And
apparently, he was now the main driving force behind
Project: AquaProductivity.

'This is supposed to make us do more work, isn't it?'
Rose said.

'Hm?'

'The water.'

'Probably. It's like, maybe it'll go away if we sell more.
Shall we try?'

Siobhan picked up the receiver of the clunky late-90s
phone sitting in front of her. It had a twisted cord that
she could play with and thread between her fingers when
she talked.

'Yes, hello, is this Mr Turner? This is Siobhan, from

MoneyTownCashGrowth, do you remember us? Yes, you bought some Promises and Bonds from us last year. How are those doing?'

Rose watched the water level intently. It was lapping at the legs of her desk. Every time someone walked past outside, it rocked slowly.

Siobhan's customer sounded pleased with what she was saying and he bought some more Shares, Bonds and Promises, which would be shipped out later that day. They watched the water level for any change. No, it seemed to stay the same. Maybe one wasn't enough. Maybe it needed to go up by, like, a thousand.

A soft knock on the door. Lynn stuck her head into the office. 'Siobhan? I was wondering if I could have a word, please.'

'Sure,' Siobhan double-clicked something on her computer screen and pushed her chair back, making waves in the water and grooves in the carpet floor.

They stepped out into the hallway, leaving the door partially closed. Rose pushed her chair closer to the door – with minimal splashing sounds – and tried to breathe extra quietly so she'd be able to hear what they were talking about.

'I see you have a friend,' said Lynn. Rose could imagine her lips pursing up into a sharp point.

'Yes. His name is Sterlington. He's my dog,' said Siobhan. She was probably crossing her arms in front of her chest.

'I don't remember you having a dog before,' said Lynn.

'I've had him for years. It's just I'm not normally based in the office for the whole day like this,' said Siobhan.

'Did you get permission to keep a dog in your office?

Just out of curiosity. Just wondering,' said Lynn, clearly not just wondering.

There was a pause. A silence.

Rose held her breath.

'No, I didn't realise I had to. He was always with me when I went to visit clients. It's never been a problem,' said Siobhan. Rose was picturing her mouth tightening around the words.

'Well, you're here now. You'd better go talk to Evan. I want nothing to do with this.'

'Sure.'

There was another silence. Rose thought she might pass out if she kept holding her breath, but she didn't dare make a sound in case she missed something.

'Was there anything else?' said Siobhan, her tone dripping with the pretence of politeness.

'No, that's all. Thanks!' said Lynn. As she said the last word Rose could hear her move away through the corridor towards her office.

Siobhan came back in and Rose quickly splashed over to the window. The city was bright and its grey walls had a glow.

'Did you send it?' Siobhan asked. She looked rattled.

Rose didn't know what to do. She didn't know if she should be asking how Siobhan was doing; it felt oddly intimate.

'No. I'll have to have another read. I don't even know what I'm saying. It's not like we'll get an explanation. It'd be good if I could ask for something.'

'I have an idea.'

From: relli@moneytowncashgrowth.co.uk
To: ehump@moneytowncashgrowth.co.uk
Subject: Flooding

Dear Mr Humperdink,

As I am sure you are aware, the fourth floor of the building seems to be flooded. It is therefore necessary to wear protective footwear. As this is an expense directly related to the recent flooding, I feel it is appropriate to approach you with a request for help with acquiring said protective footwear.

I have attached a document listing some links to cost-effective, yet still professional-looking, footwear. The delivery is speedy as well.

Thank you very much,
Best wishes,
Rose

'You could make a spreadsheet with everyone's shoe size,' Siobhan said and stretched. Sterlington yawned.

'Good.'

Rose splashed out the door and into every office, taking down people's shoe sizes. Most just responded obediently, but a few questioned her motives. Surely it wasn't necessary to wear wellies to the office? What would that look like? They weren't working in an actual swamp, it was just a bit of water! It was important to keep appearing professional.

It was 3:55pm when she got back to her office. Rose thought about the well-known fact that the hour from three to four is the longest hour in any one day of work. She pulled up Excel, made a spreadsheet. Made a table for shoe size and colour preference, then colour-coded it and sorted it by size, price, delivery options, carbon impact of ordering from overseas, and the long-term benefit of buying high quality footwear. She made a graph. Made a pie chart. Made it look good.

4:30pm.

There.

'Now shall I send it?'

'With the spreadsheet? Definitely.'

Bye, Trevor at reception. Thank you. See you later! Siobhan put Sterlington on his leash and carried him to Lift 2. There was a notice on Lift 1 saying Floor 4 staff weren't allowed to use it because the water would splash down into the lower floor. It was full of people from the top floors whose faces revealed panic and worry about their shoes and the bottoms of their trousers. The doors, which opened and closed quickly, let a few inches of water into the lift, a collective gasp resounded, and the staff of Floor 4 shared a knowing look. Psh, a bit of water for a second in the lift? Try walking through it all day!

A bond developed, then, between Rose and her colleagues. Just a little bit. It was forged by a glance down at opaque black tights soaked to the ankle, or the dry shoes held in a colleague's hand, his stripy red and white socks on display.

On her way home through the Meadows, Rose started to miss the comfort of being around other soggy trouser hems. She had become the odd one out, walking down a street in Marchmont immersed in a crowd of completely dry-looking people. They looked at her with polite interest, but turned their heads away quickly. They probably thought she'd stood in a very deep puddle, one they themselves would certainly have had the common sense to avoid.

A few blocks from her flat, Rose's phone buzzed with a text message.

HEY GRL HW R U CN U PCK UP MILK PLS? Jx

Josh. She sighed, feeling irritation bubble up in her throat. Fine. She could pick up the milk. Never mind the fact that she'd spent the entire day in wet socks and her brogues were definitely ruined. She also had to pick up milk.

At the corner shop she handed over a damp fiver to the person at the till, who handled it with his fingertips, dried it off on his sleeve and shot her a wary look. She half expected him to pour his Diet Coke over her change in retaliation, but he didn't. The coins were dry. Accusingly so. She pocketed the change and walked towards home.

Josh rarely ate anything other than cereal and Rose supplied the milk to keep up his habit. She hardly ever used it herself. She was an enabler.

The whole walk home the milk carton was cold in her grip, and beaded with water. She unlocked the door with her other hand, and the stale air – brand *Josh had the day off today* – wafted towards her.

'Thank you for the milk, Rose, you're a star,' said Josh. He hadn't even checked if she had got it – he just assumed.

'It's fine, don't worry about it,' said Rose. She walked into the kitchen, waved across the hall into the living room where Josh was perched on the sofa in his normal owl-like position, and put the milk in the fridge next to several bulging cartons of orange juice, all way past their use-by date, all too explosive to handle.

Rose went to her bedroom, which meant she had to walk through the living room and past Josh.

'Did it rain?' he asked. He wasn't the most observant of characters, but even a non-observant person would have noticed the distinct squelch of wet shoes. Rose hadn't been certain, up until that moment, whether she was going to tell him or not. But his small comment made all that worry disappear.

'Oh God, Josh,' she threw up her arms in theatrical despair, and dropped her weary body into the threadbare beanbag by the TV.

'What did I do?' he asked.

'It's not you,' she said. And she told him about the water, the email, Lynn, the little paper ship. The whole thing.

'Shit,' he said after she finished.

'I know,' she said.

'What are you going to do?' he asked.

'I don't know. Maybe it'll go away. Maybe it'll be okay. They can't do this forever, can they?' she said.

He drew in a deep breath and launched into a lengthy speech about the joys of working in hospitality and the lack of corporate bullshit he had to deal with, which Rose knew for a fact was 100% fictitious because Josh worked for a large multinational coffee chain and had quite a lot of corporate bullshit thrown his way. It was just a different brand of corporate bullshit.

Rose zoned out. She didn't feel bad about doing this; she'd been living with Josh for the past two years, and they'd had enough of these types of chats for them both to know what they were in for. She'd whine about her life, he'd lecture her, neither would really listen to the other person, and then they'd go about their merry way.

WEDNESDAY

Rose went to work to find that the water level had risen and Trevor had changed his hair. Both were mildly unsettling. It took Rose a good few trips past Trevor's desk to realise that he had just parted his hair on the other side, making his face look like a mirror image of itself.

Rose found that Sterlington made for an entertaining addition to room 4.02. It was fun to watch him fight his own instincts, torn between wanting to jump up and watch Siobhan's computer screen and the intense need to never ever touch the watery floor. Having Siobhan back was also nice. After a few hours in her dazzling presence Rose could even muster what amounted to regular-sounding small talk without blushing or fretting about saying the wrong thing.

For about a week, the water level stayed the same. The fourth floor started settling into a strange routine, measuring sales success in lines drawn in pencil on white walls, like parents marking the growth of a child.

FRIDAY

After a week of barely perceptible change, the water suddenly went up to Rose's knees. It was a hot day, and humid, so the water was quite refreshing. There was still no response from Evan on the top floor. Evan, with his dry feet, was probably roasting and wouldn't have minded a dip in the new company pool on level four. Well, Evan, that pool is yours whenever you want it, thought Rose, glancing up at the top floor as she approached the building.

All shoes were off. There was no trace of the wellingtons Rose had requested. Everyone just took their shoes off in Lift 2 and left them with Trevor at reception. Trevor was not pleased about this. Rose heard that he requested some storage boxes to keep the shoes in, but hadn't heard anything back. Typical. Maybe Evan needed a personal assistant to help him keep on top of the emails. Rose didn't want that job. She'd rather wade through water every day.

The water was making the swivelly chairs float now, all foam seats and hollow plastic, so you had to sit down and never get up. You'd walk into your office and find your chair floating there on its back, like a leisurely swimmer, and you'd have to pull it towards you, tilt it slightly and get on it when its feet were pointing downwards. The rubbish bins became flotsam, so those who would prefer them to stay underneath their desks parked their legs on top of them to hold them down, or weighed them down with staplers, hole punches or stones. The stones had to be brought in from outside, as no one had any stones just lying around their office, with the exception of Robert's neighbour Timothy, who had had a stone on his desk since he started. It had served as a paperweight until that Friday, when it was converted into an instant bin-weight instead. Everyone in the big office was very jealous.

From: lmerc@moneytowncashgrowth.co.uk
To: All Staff
CC: ehump@moneytowncashgrowth.co.uk
Subject: Review ongoing

Dear Colleague,

As you'll no doubt have noticed, the review of our ongoing Sales Improvement through water has not yet been completed, so the next stage of the project has begun, resulting in a higher volume of water on the premises.

Many thanks,
Lynn Mercer, Regional Sales Division Director

Rose had finally found a reason to start wearing the array of pencil skirts her mum had given her when she started this job. In a skirt of a certain length she still looked vaguely professional, and didn't really have to change her attire all that much. If she had kept wearing trousers she might have had to deal with Robert or Trevor's issues, who left the office every night with legs soaked all the way up to their knees. Shoes abandoned, everyone still looked the way they had looked before, but trouser wearers had started to walk more slowly, their legs dragging wet fabric. Shorts would've probably been unacceptable – but no one had pushed it that far yet.

Not everyone had abandoned shoes. Obviously, Lynn still wore heels. She now had a preference towards those with little straps at the top because she kept losing the others. It was incredible how she could walk with her back perfectly straight while obviously straining against the volumes of water around her.

Then Friday was over. Well, the working day. A wave of water rode the lift down with Rose and spilled into the lobby of the building.

The weekend was upon Rose. She could think of nothing but going to the beach and of having her friends over that evening. She'd been holding back, texting vague *Work is annoying* messages back and forth but not getting down to business yet. She was saving that until she saw them in person.

That night, Josh was out with friends, escaping from an escape room, and Madison and Hanna came over. Madison brought cheeses and they ate them while watching *Vertigo* and drinking wine. Hanna had to be up early in the morning for a design review on her latest building plan so she kept checking the PDF on her phone to make sure she hadn't missed out any windows. Apparently, windows were important. This was her second year of university and she was determined not to mess up.

Madison worked at MoneyGrowthTownCash, a similar company to Rose's, which dealt not in Promises, but in Excuses. Rose had bought one of them early on in Madison's career, just after Madison quit MoneyTownCashGrowth. It was framed above Rose's TV.

```
        'I'm sorry
        but I had
    something better
        to do'
```

Madison had made it herself. This was before she started moving up in MoneyGrowthTownCash and, consequently, taking her job a bit more seriously. The Excuse even had the professional logo on it and everything. Madison had printed it after hours and charged Rose a tequila shot and a slice of pizza for it. Sometimes, Rose looked up at the certificate and thought, yes, yes, I do.

Today, Madison was a married lady, a proper adult. Rose still wasn't over it, even though they'd known each other now for how many years?

'How long have we known each other?'

Madison was eating a cracker and some Stilton.

'Eight.'

'No, nine,' said Rose.

'Nine years,' Madison said. Hanna had her PDF open again.

'That's right. Wow, we're old.'

'Can you look at this, does it look crooked? It doesn't look crooked, right?' Hanna waved the phone in front of their faces.

'Honey, you drew the lines on the computer. They wouldn't be crooked. There's probably no way they can be. It's fine.'

None of Hanna's designs had ever been made into a building. This was a floor plan for CashGrowthMoneyTown's new headquarters, or, more specifically, for their 'leisure and relaxation' facilities. They'd probably call it LeizLax@Cash or some equally vile portemanteau, thought Rose.

'What's that bit?'

'Laundry room.'

'Why do they need a laundry room?' Madison dipped the half-cracker in some onion jam in a tiny mason jar that she'd brought along in true Madison fashion.

'It's convenient.'

'Yeah, but how does that count as relaxation?' said Rose. She was a little tipsy.

'Or *leisure*?' said Madison. She was also a little tipsy.

'Well,' Hanna braced herself. 'Actually, you'll find that you're more *relaxed* when you don't have to worry about having to do your laundry after work. So this way, you can just do it *at work* and get it done!'

The two others snorted into their wine glasses.

Hanna looked upset and checked the potentially crooked line again.

Rose thought about using Hanna's experience to segue into what had happened to her, by saying something like, Hah, you think a laundry room will make them less stressed out? *Try removing the inches of water they have to wade through*, but then remembered that it was probably a company secret and not for her friends to know. Plus, they'd just tell her to quit her job, and she couldn't be having that conversation again.

At one point, all of them had worked at MoneyTownCashGrowth. They had all started there, and Rose was the only one who was still in the same place. It was petty, she knew, but she didn't want to give up just to move to a similar job at a different company. If she ever left – which she would, once she found something better, she thought, the wine oversaturating the colours around her – it would be to make a dramatic change. But she couldn't possibly tell Madison and Hanna about that.

They might've talked her out of it, or made her do it.

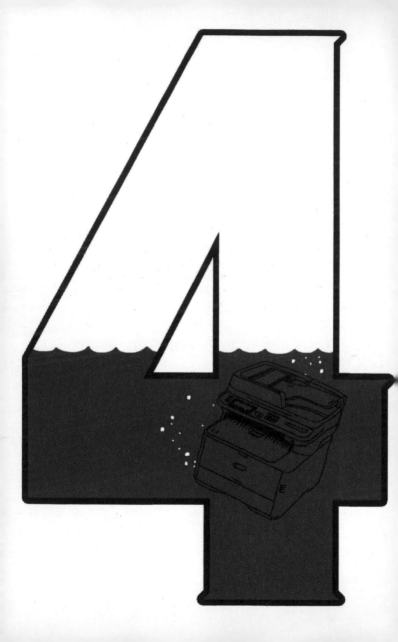

SATURDAY

Saturday was beach day.

Rose liked to take the train out to Dunbar and spend the entirety of Saturday catching waves, even though it could be quite choppy. The occasional rainfall made the entire experience wet from all sides, but nothing was better than tasting salt all day and eating a chip shop supper before heading back, hair crusty, eyes burning, tired all through her body.

Rose arrived with all her things at 9am. She liked that the train ride was short because it meant she only had to inconvenience her fellow passengers with the sheer bulk of her surfing gear for twenty minutes. Walking past the surf school, Rose felt slightly superior to the queue of people waiting to hire a light-weight beginner's board. Never mind that hers was also far from heavy – at least she owned it. The cord was wound tightly along the shape of the board as she carried it, but with every step the loop loosened, until finally the ankle strap slapped against the surface of the board, the cord slid off, and its end hopped along the pavement beside Rose. She gathered it up. Her face was red. No one had noticed.

As Rose pulled on her wetsuit in the public toilet by the rocks she smacked herself in the eye with her knuckle. The fabric had been sticking to her skin too much, and she'd lost her grip as she pulled it up her arm. She saw white spots for a second, then it hurt.

Rose left her clothes and bags with Steve at the beachside café and waded out through the long stretch of flooded grass. A fresh wetsuit made her feel like a dolphin in the water, but on dry land, or in the places in between the two that were neither here nor there, she felt closer to a cardboard cut-out of a person, not really able to bend her knees or swing her hips. Even though it was a weekend, she found it hard not to think about the office, especially now, with the water splashing at her calves. Trying to push the parallels away, she decided that this was a wetness she had chosen, which was therefore completely contrary to the water at the office.

Finally, it got deep enough for her to let go of her board and let it float next to her, her hand flat on it, feeling its movements and guiding it. As she waded further out the board flattened the long blades of grass. Her feet were sinking into the ground. Rose upped her pace to get into the deeper water, so she wouldn't have time to think about what might be moving underneath the soles of her feet. The ground squelched and released bubbles with every step she took.

Rose's research had confirmed that working on a boat wouldn't be as easy as she'd previously assumed, but that couldn't stop her from looking at boats from afar as she waded through the sea.

There it was. She was out in the open. She dove once,

twice, to wet her hair and get her face accustomed to the cold, then got on the board and swam a bit further out. She liked that it was hard and flat underneath her, with a familiar rough surface, and that the waves either side of it felt silky in comparison.

Rose hopped off, one arm still on the board, and looked out to the sea. It was a sunny day and the water was brilliant and clear.

Was that a wave? She had trouble telling.

That was a wave rolling towards her, she decided.

She paddled herself around, facing the beach, heaved herself onto the board, her toes bent against the bottom edge, and checked again behind her.

Should she start swimming?

She started swimming, tentatively, with her fingers brushing the water to check for currents. She was lucky, there were lots of currents, but she just couldn't be sure if they were the right ones.

Damn it. Why did she go alone?

She swam harder now, not wanting to turn around to check if the wave was approaching in case it would suck her under.

It crashed behind her, too soon, and she spat frothy water as it dissipated before it reached her, the sea around her boiling in tiny swirls, white and blue.

Rose slipped off the board, treading water. She licked her lips, squinted out to the beach, then grabbed the board again, turned it around, and drifted back out to where she had been.

She could always try again.

Once, twice, she caught one. It lifted her all the way,

carried her to dry land, and the strokes of her arms were one with the beat of the tide. She couldn't tell whether it was luck or skill, but she suspected the truth probably lay somewhere in the middle.

And then it was time to go home.

Rose sucked a salty strand of hair on the way home on the train. Her limbs ached. She'd gone alone, again, because her surfing buddies Rachael and Drew had moved away to Australia. She liked looking at their pictures of sunrise surfing and yoga, which were inspiring and annoying in equal parts. It still stung, and felt like a personal sleight, that they had left her; even though she knew they were happy there and that Rachael was glad to be back home. Anyway, it had been six months; time to get over it.

After her shower, Rose settled down in front of the TV with a bag of marshmallows. The marshmallows had no fat, which meant they were healthy. Rose had bought them by accident and they did taste faintly of polystyrene but there were no others snacks in the house. Josh was at the coffee shop still, and she revelled in the hours of quiet. She watched a show about Greece and its islands. She felt restless, like little wings were shifting and itching underneath her shoulder blades, and she counted how many days of holiday she still had left for the year. Ten. That's enough. Except she'd need a couple of them for Christmas, and she might also want to go away in autumn when the city got colourful and rainy. With her legs tucked up underneath her, she leaned forwards on the sofa and grabbed a notepad from the coffee table.

Ten. Three for Christmas. Maybe two.

Eight. Two for autumn, for a long weekend in the Lake

District or something.

Rose tapped her pen on the paper and calculated. It would take a few hours to get there. Yes.

Six. She could take six.

Maybe save one for an emergency.

She drew a squiggle before she put the final figure down.

Five.

Greece.

And she could work on a boat. Maybe she would ask Siobhan to come along. That might be nice. She started drafting a text to her but then didn't know how to ask it without feeling like she was asking too much too soon. She'd mention it in the office, she decided.

Then Rose thought of Monday, which was closer now that Saturday was over. She'd have to call clients again. Evan probably still wouldn't have responded to her email about the waterproof boots. Siobhan might still be tied to her desk, with the money for field work no longer available. Maybe Sterlington would be back. A small tingle in her stomach. Rose ate four marshmallows. The faint choking sensation and sugar rush pushed the boredom she was anticipating to the back of her mind.

The ad break was over. Greece was back on the screen. It was all turquoise and whole lambs roasting on spits, ceramics and white walls, large pitchers of wine. Rose stretched out and rested her legs on the table, a pillow in her lap, and ate another marshmallow.

Monday. Greece. The boat.

SUNDAY

Sunday passed with a phone call from her mother and a visit to IKEA. Rose thought she might need another lamp, but it turned out that she needed a pack of batteries, three scented candles, a decorative rug *and* another lamp. She also did some laundry and left it to dry on a clotheshorse. Looking at the skirts and button-down shirts drying there, she thought about how high the water level might be on Monday, and how pointless it was to wash and dry clothes anyway. Still, shouldn't lose hope. Got to keep that hope up. Got to keep everything ticking over like normal.

How high would it be? Knees?

Thighs?

Did it keep rising on weekends, or did Evan make it go away so the cleaners could hoover the floors? Rose had a quick vision of cleaners vacuuming up all the water from the floor into a big tank, then refilling it once they were done, like pool maintenance.

Rose's mother had asked about work, but Rose didn't say anything about the water. It just didn't come up.

'How's work going?'

'It's fine.'

'Is Siobhan still gone?'

'Why do you ask?'

'Just wondering, dear.'

'She's back.'

'That's nice. A bit of companionship.'

'Yeah,' Rose felt embarrassed but didn't know why.

Not even once did her mother say, 'Any water-related changes to your working environment, dear?' Besides, it was just a company measure, boring office stuff. Different font in the company letterheads, Trevor's new hair, office flooded.

MONDAY

Monday. Time just kept moving forward and kept spitting out another Monday.

Rose's shower time pep talk went around in circles – it'll be fine, it's not fine, you could just not go, but you can't just not show up. Only when she was satisfied that all her pores were wide open and her hair extremely clean did she step out of the shower. The bath mat was soaking wet, so Rose stepped over it to the comparatively dry tiles, thinking, again, that taking a shower was a bit pointless. Sure, her top half would probably not be submerged, but she thought she might like to swim around instead of walking upright.

She'd be faster.

She'd be the fastest down the corridor, the first to the kitchen.

Just in case, she picked a black blouse. Not white – that'd be obscene.

Sure enough, Lynn was wearing her normal outfit. Rose met her in the lift, and she noted that, up to that point, Lynn had definitely looked more like someone about to go to an office: top knot, pearls, white blouse, high-waisted skirt down to her knees, stockings, heels. Rose, on the other hand, was wearing a black blouse and some yoga trousers she hoped didn't look like yoga trousers, but which absolutely looked like yoga trousers. And she didn't even do yoga. These were just very comfortable trousers.

The lift doors opened onto the fourth floor, and with a gasp Rose felt that the water was up to her hips. They were really pumping more in. The water was cool and didn't seem dirty, and it smelled of the sea. After ten days of this, it was still hard to believe it was really happening. This was her life now. From now on, she'd only have dry feet before 9am.

Lynn dropped her arms to hold her skirt down. Its material had started drifting, lifting. Trevor was sitting at reception, his keyboard floating above the desk in front of him. He grinned at Lynn and Rose, wished them a good morning and handed Lynn some wet letters that had arrived for her. She walked off to her corner office, the letters wedged under her arm as she clung on to the seam of her skirt, pushing it down and against her legs.

'The technicians are coming at 10, so clear your desk,' said Trevor.

'What's happening now?' Rose was irritated. She thought the cablers had already finished their work.

He waved his hand at the keyboard and pushed it back down onto the desk to demonstrate the issue. With the water splashing about a foot above desk-level, the keyboard kept floating away whenever he removed his typing fingers. 'This is a nightmare.'

'See you later,' she said. Technicians.

Before heading to her office, Rose went into the kitchen to get a cup of tea and maybe a biscuit if Robert had left any.

He had.

They were in the top drawer of the kitchen unit, still in their packet, encased in a practical Tupperware box. Rose could've kissed Robert for being so sensible. She was sure that the biscuits were the only dry thing in that kitchen. With her affection still high, she felt bad taking biscuits from him. She only ate one. Stealing Robert's biscuits was a time-honoured tradition.

Siobhan was behind her desk when Rose waded in. She fought the urge to let her body sink in just a tiny bit more, pulling her legs away from the ground, and paddling herself around the room. Instead, she resisted, and walked. Her yoga trousers were nice and snug, and they offered little resistance to the water, so her walk was more of a slow glide. She shovelled out a handful of water and splashed Siobhan on the back of her chair.

'Why?' Siobhan said. She didn't even turn around.

Rose shrugged, and felt a warm comfort in the pit of her stomach.

They were all wet anyway, it didn't really matter anymore. Siobhan was wedged under her desk, but it had begun to float ever so slightly, rocking itself, and Siobhan with it, back and forth, side to side. The wave Rose had created by walking in through the door pushed Siobhan ever so slightly to the back of the room, closer to the windows, before the wave crashed against the wall and brought her back again.

Rose waded over to her own desk. Everything on it, the

keyboard, the stapler, the paper clips – she liked to pile them up to make a tower – and the mouse, was floating.

A knock on the door.

A man in blue overalls came splashing in, soaking wet, from his submerged feet to his dripping strands of dark hair. He was wearing goggles that covered half his face, with a bright green snorkel, the mouthpiece poking him in the cheek.

'Here to sort out the desks,' he said. His voice sounded funny with his nose encased in rubber.

'Hi, Jon!' said Siobhan. She smiled and pushed herself back from her desk in a nonchalant twirly motion. The chair didn't want to follow her lead, so she ended up on her back, sinking, gasping. Jon waded over to her and pulled her out of the water, back into a standing position. She was dripping wet - her blush melted off her face, and her swoopy fringe stuck to her forehead.

Rose didn't laugh, but she had to bite her tongue really hard. Was this what Siobhan's flirting style looked like?

Jon crouched down in front of Siobhan's desk, put the snorkel in his mouth, and ducked underwater. All that remained of him on the surface was a little green snorkel, its opening dangerously close to the surface of the water. It moved side to side while Jon worked. Siobhan was standing by the window, wringing out her long hair. With it all wet like that rather than floaty and bouncy, Rose noted that Siobhan's face looked fragile and small.

Then Jon reappeared and grabbed a power drill from inside his jacket, which he had draped over Sterlington's chair – Sterlington had taken the morning off. Jon sank to his knees and plugged the drill into the socket behind the chair. Once again Rose thought of the electricity and the cables, half-expecting all the lights to zap out and a flash of lightning to zig-zag across the room.

Nothing.

Jon dove from the chair to his position underneath Siobhan's desk and drilled four holes through the desk, then reappeared and attached her keyboard to the desk's surface with four efficient screws. All the while, Siobhan's wireless mouse was floating around in the general vicinity.

'There's a plan for these as well.'

As if he had been waiting for his cue, another man in blue appeared in the doorway. Rose thought that he had probably been lurking around in the hall so as not to crowd the office too much.

Jon greeted the second man by saying 'Hiya, mate', so Rose was unable to deduce what his name was. He was carrying a big sack over his shoulder, which made him look like a thin, blue Santa. Once the sack was dumped in the water, the man opened it and took out two small creels with fluorescent netting bent around a neat wooden base.

'Are we getting pets for the office?'

'No,' said Jon. He pounced on Siobhan's mouse, which had been drifting in the water above her desk, pointing its red light downwards and sending the cursor on Siobhan's computer screen flying around. Then he opened the creel, caught the mouse inside and drilled the creel to the surface of the desk.

'You're next,' he said.

Rose felt vaguely threatened.

Both men busied themselves underneath her desk while she stood by Siobhan, watching the swirling water and the electrical appliances in it.

When it came to finishing the final drilling from underneath the table top, they just pulled off their snorkels, took a large breath, and dove. Every time one of them ran out of air, the other one would take over, making for a seamless sort of power drill relay race. When they finished, they didn't stop to admire their handiwork, just unplugged the power drill and packed up their things.

'Right, that's us done now!'

'Cheers, thanks for that! Bye, Jon,' said Siobhan and Rose, waving from the window. Their desks looked oddly normal now that their keyboards weren't floating around.

Both men waved and left. They might've both been called Jon, thought Rose. She sat back down at her desk and tapped on the space key to bring her screen back to life.

Now Siobhan and Rose had two lobster creels sitting on their desks, with mice inside them. There was a hole at the front for them to stick their hands through, and this way they wouldn't float off and down the hallway. It was great.

Siobhan sat back down and picked up her phone, which had also been drilled to the desk. She dialled a number underwater, and then started selling a company in London a big, expensive Promise.

Rose took a step back from her desk, and then sank down to the floor. Her chest, her shoulders, her ears were submerged, and then she tilted her face and it, too, dipped underneath the surface of the water.

She held her breath.

She opened her eyes.

From within the water, the office looked like a strange aquarium.

The bottom half of her computer screen looked the same as it always had, just sort of wobbly and wet.

Cool.

She came back up for breath, smoothed her hair behind her ears, sat down to get to work, sell some Promises and splash Siobhan around the side of their desks.

Robert came over in his lunch break and challenged Rose to a butterfly contest in the hallway. There was someone there to make sure no one would see, and Siobhan agreed to be the timekeeper. Robert won, but Rose put it down to experience. She explained to Siobhan that if there had been crashing waves and a natural current and the competition had been in surfing and not swimming, she would have totally nailed it. Siobhan nodded but didn't look very convinced.

That day at 5pm, getting into the lift felt like they were all coming home from Saturday morning swimming practice, which made Rose hungry for some cinnamon sugar toast, the way her auntie had always made it when she was little. The water trapped inside the lift flooded the lobby again and it stood there, an inch high, for them to splash through on their way to the revolving doors, where they pushed it out into the street, one triangular segment at a time.

Rose stood on a corner of Tollcross Mansion and spilled a purse-full of water onto the pavement while she looked for change. She was going to treat herself to a bus ride.

Maybe. If she found change.

'Yes, I'm fine,' she said into her phone.

'I saw Frank the other day,' said Rose's mum.

Rose rolled her eyes and made a noise.

'He looked nice. He finally stopped wearing those loafers everywhere.' As if the loafers had been the only thing that was wrong with Frank. *Frank.* 'He's still going out with Nina, you know. Nice girl.'

Rose made another noise. It came out through her nose.

'Are you grunting at me, pet?'

'No.' Now Rose's eyes hurt from being rolled so dramatically, so she just squeezed them shut instead.

'Anyway, Frank and Nina were looking good. They asked after you.'

'Yeah?'

'And I said, well, she's doing really well, thank you, and she's working for a big bank, I think.' Rose nodded, even though her mum couldn't see. 'Anyway, that's nice, isn't it?'

'Yes.'

After the conversation was over, Rose checked her purse again and couldn't find any change. She did, however, find a shiny button and a wet receipt. She put her phone in her jacket breast pocket, which made her want to put a pocket square there too, and perhaps an array of fountain pens.

When the Sales Team had all left together, the waterlogged clothing up to their belly buttons had marked them as colleagues. Comrades. But now that Floor 4 staff were all dispersed across the city and she was by herself outside the building Rose found herself feeling quite damp, cold and alone. Her yoga trousers had soaked up all the water, making them clammy and horrible with all that wind blowing around her. She tried really hard not to feel embarrassed, to feel comforted by the knowledge that her colleagues all had to deal with the same issue, but it all caught up with her and she blushed whenever she felt someone stare at her wet clothes.

The conversation with her mum had taken so long that even those of her colleagues who worked till 5:05, 5:15, or the especially eager 5:30 ones had left. She was the only one left.

She wanted a towel.

And she wanted to not be wet.

Maybe it was then, or even earlier that day, that she considered bringing a change of clothes to the office. It would require extra effort, but it would mean that she wouldn't have to ride the bus like this or walk down the street looking like there had been a surprise bit of rain confined to just her, soaking her body from her belly button downwards. You know, that common kind of very specialised rain.

On her phone, she typed out another quick email to Evan Humperdink, who still hadn't responded to any of her previous messages.

From: relli@moneytowncashgrowth.co.uk
To: ehump@moneytowncashgrowth.co.uk
Subject: Lockers?

Dear Mr Humperdink,
Regarding our general situation (re: flooding of floor 4) it might be advisable to invest in lockers for

```
the lobby to facilitate keeping a
change of clothes on site.

Best,
Rose
```

She sent it. Then she walked home. It probably wouldn't happen.

Her routine upon returning home had shifted, and she could already feel it becoming commonplace instead of sort of novel and exciting. Rather than toeing off her shoes and walking around in her socks for an hour, her first instinct was to head straight to the bathroom, where she peeled off her wet trousers and socks and draped them over the shower rail. Then she towelled off and slipped into her pyjama bottoms and some woolly socks. In June.

Josh was home, and asked about the office, like he'd done every day since she had confided in him. She felt a deep sort of regret about telling him, the kind of regret she imagined was normally reserved for letting your real personality loose at an office party.

There was a pizza in the oven now. It had materialised from the depths of the freezer and after she peeled off the ice crystals and the plastic wrap, she deemed it acceptable. While she ate it, watching TV with Josh, she considered calling Madison but decided against it. She wondered if the news had made its way to her yet, that MoneyTownCashGrowth was in trouble, or at least Rose's department.

There was another documentary on TV, and Rose fell asleep thinking of climbing a glacier. When she woke up, chilly, she found that Josh had draped a blanket over her.

Maybe it wasn't so bad. Maybe she didn't regret sharing bits about her life with him.

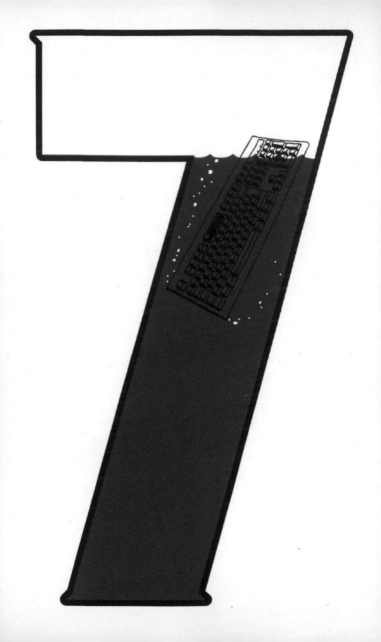

TUESDAY

The next day the water level was the same. It hadn't changed. Though some said it was lower.

'Don't you feel like the water has gone down a bit?' said Robert, scratching his head with a long finger.

'Yeah,' said Rose. And it did feel like it had. 'Maybe we're doing better?'

'I think everyone's been trying a bit harder.'

'No shit.'

'No, but seriously, I feel like we're going to be okay. I feel like it's going to go away.'

'Bit of a shame,' said Rose, and kicked up a wave onto Robert's shirt.

Siobhan had slushed up and was now leaning in the hallway against the wall next to Rose. She looked at her hands. 'It smells funny in here,' she noted, and picked at a cuticle.

The three of them paused in their tracks and inhaled collectively through their noses.

Robert took a step closer to call them into his confidence. 'Someone's been saying that Jim hasn't left his chair to go to the bathroom. Like, he just sits there. All day. Without getting up. To go to the bathroom.'

He tilted his sharp chin up to let the words take effect.

Siobhan and Rose shuddered, which sent the tiniest ripple through the hallway. The water lapped at the wallpaper which was going green with algae.

'That's it. I'm going up there to tell Evan that this is unacceptable,' said Siobhan, and turned around for what was planned to be a dramatically brisk exit. Her pace was slowed down, however, by the water. She strained against the waves, but that only made it worse, as each rushed attempt to push forward sent another wave crashing against the door and pushed her back.

'Well, there's nothing we can do,' said Robert.

'Why not? We made the water go down!' Siobhan slapped the surface of the water and made small concentric ripples.

'Well, we made it not rise,' Rose said. 'We think. I don't think we've got much influence here.'

She knew that sharing an office and a part-time dog meant that she should be on Siobhan's side, but this was ridiculous. They wouldn't even cause a stir. Siobhan would go up to Evan's office, dripping and smelling of the sea, and he'd send her off with some pleasantries and no real change. And worst of all, she'd thank him for it, and feel like she really got through to him. That was the way with Evan.

'Listen. Stop. We can just talk to Jim.' Rose suggested.

And the three of them half-swam to the big office floor and circled around Jim, father of three, who was furiously typing away on his computer. He looked like the flood was really getting to him. They kept a safe distance.

'Jim.'

'Oh, hey, Rose. How's it going? Shame about the flood, isn't it?'

'Yeah. Shame.'

There was a silence. They didn't know how to approach it.

'Jim, a couple of us have been wondering whether...' Robert started, but Siobhan didn't let him finish.

'Jim, are you peeing in everyone's water?'

'What? Jesus. No!' he said and blushed to his roots 'Who's been saying that? Either way, it's not me. I can't go when there's people watching, not that that's any of your business. I'm a bit busy, can we talk about this later?'

'Suspicious,' Siobhan whispered out of the side of her mouth in Rose's direction. She made sure that Jim heard it too.

They swam back to their office, and Robert stayed for a few more minutes to chat before heading to the first floor, where their toilets were now located. Well, their own toilets were still located in the same place, but they just weren't useable anymore. Sometimes Rose still went into one of the stalls and sat down on a closed lid, for old time's sake, just to get away for a moment.

As they sat down at their desks, Siobhan took out a binder full of laminated pages and started flipping through it. That was very clever, thought Rose. She had all her files on her computer, because this was the 21st century, but the bottom half of the screen was already dipping into the water, making it difficult to hit certain icons in the control panel. She managed, but only from muscle memory, not because she could actually see them.

An email arrived. A little notification at the bottom of the screen winked up at her through the wetness.

```
From: lmerc@moneytowncashgrowth.co.uk
To: All Staff
CC: ehump@moneytowncashgrowth.co.uk
Subject: Walking

Dear all,

It has been reported that some of
our staff have ceased to take their
appearance seriously, especially
when it comes to moving through the
office in a respectable manner. I
would like to state here that it is
not appropriate to treat this space
as a swimming pool. It is a place of
work, and I expect each and every one
of our staff to be mindful of this by
walking upright at all times.

Many thanks,

Lynn Mercer
```

Rose simmered with anger. Or maybe not strictly anger, but frustration, and the need to respond with an irrational message. And an overwhelming desire to dive into the water, backstroke down the hallway to Lynn's office, and spit a fountain of salty water in her face.

But that would be childish.

Still. Walking? In Rose's mind, that was just inefficient. Her bottom and legs were perpetually wet now, and when she sat down, she was in the water up to her elbows. At least it was a decent temperature, cool enough to keep her awake.

Kerry disagreed. They went out to pick up some lunch, a group of fourth-floorers. Their walk was squishy, and they made sure to stay on pavements and paths to avoid covering their bottom halves in mud. Their watery footsteps on the concrete dried behind them as they ate sandwiches and drank coffees. This was when Kerry disagreed.

'Isn't the water *absolutely freezing?* I mean, it might just be my corner of the office, but wow, it's cold,' she said and dug a fork into a pre-packaged pasta salad.

'It's fine over where I am,' said Robert.

Rose nodded. 'Yeah, I like that it's cool.'

'Well, I'm freezing. And God knows Lynn won't do anything about it,' said Kerry.

'Oh, don't tell her,' said Rose. She preferred to settle things with her colleagues and leave Lynn out of it. Especially because Lynn would just refer them on to Evan, who was useless and never responded to emails.

'I wasn't going to,' said Kerry, pointing with her plastic container. 'I think I might bring my kettle. You know, plug it in, heat up some of that water.'

'You'd better talk to Jim about that, he's right next to you,' said Rose, and Robert turned around and looked at her with eyes that seemed to say, *Don't mention the peeing or Kerry will go nuts.* Well, his eyes just sort of squinted a bit and stared in a weird, piercing manner, but Rose imagined that's what he wanted to say.

Kerry nodded.

Robert told them about his five-a-side football match on Saturday, and how important this one was. He'd been part of the team for as long as Rose had known him, and, judging from what he had told her, they weren't very good. She nodded and said she might make it to the pub for after-game drinks this week, although she knew she'd be out surfing again.

'The thing about five-a-side is,' started Robert. Rose took a long sip from her cup of miso soup. Robert always had a lot to say about what exactly the thing about five-a-side was. His blue button-down shirt stuck to his body and you could see the outline of his white undershirt. The brown leather belt around his skinny waist was drenched too, going a deeper, unhealthy colour, slick and crackling on the sides.

'You know I tried it the other day,' Kerry confided in both of the others. She was oblivious to the fact that Robert still hadn't finished his thesis on what the thing about five-a-side was.

'Tried what?' asked Rose, while Robert finished his sentence quietly and ground the remaining words to dust with his bony jaws.

'The water,' she paused for effect. The other two kept walking, staring at the path and at Kerry's face with equal levels of interest.

'I was thirsty, but the water cooler is all the way out where Trevor is, and I didn't fancy a chat, and I was quite thirsty. And besides, the water cooler is under water now anyway, so it wouldn't have mattered. Anyway,' she took a deep breath, drew out all her syllables for the big reveal, 'I just dipped my cup in the water, because it looks clean enough, right?'

'Except for the algae,' said Rose.

'Yeah, except for the algae. So I tried it!' Kerry cried triumphantly.

Rose hid in a sip of miso soup.

'And it was really salty!'

Rose and Robert nodded.

'You knew about that?' asked Kerry. She appeared upset that her clever observation wasn't generating a bigger, more excited response.

'Well, it smells like the sea when you wring it out,' said Rose. And it did. Every night when she got home she wrung out her clothes, left them to dry and her bathroom smelled of the ocean.

Rose let Kerry walk on ahead to catch up with some Floor 2 colleagues. She stayed behind, giggling with Robert, the kinds of giggles that bubble up in your throat and make it so you can't even look the other person in the eye anymore.

When they got back after lunch, the water was the same level. They slid through the hallway triumphantly, like three little yachts, carving an elegant pattern into the surface.

A commotion. Agitated voices from the big office.

'What's going on?' she said as she reached the door. Timothy was splashing around in the back of the room looking distraught. Jim walked up to Rose and murmured, 'Rhian's gone.'

'What do you mean, gone? She was in this morning!'

'Yeah, but she's been let go.'

'They can't do that, just like that! What about a notice period?'

Spikes of waves came from Robert digging through Rhian's desk, flipping through documents, opening drawers. 'This doesn't make any sense!'

'She's been sleeping a bit,' said Jim in a low voice. 'She said the water made her feel like she was in a spa, all cosy and relaxed.'

Rose was about to pass on a triumphant remark to Robert about the appropriate water temperature, but she felt that this wasn't the time to act superior.

'Fuck.'

'And she hasn't been pulling her weight. That's what the shark said.'

'The what?'

'There was a shark in here?' said Kerry, who had now joined them. Her face was red and her hands were in woollen mittens.

'Yeah, I mean, he was only in for a second, so I couldn't really see, but I definitely think it was a shark. He was wearing a suit,' Jim added.

'We missed a shark?!' said Rose, and did a twirl in exasperation. The water around her legs swirled in a little maelstrom, sucking up two paper clips and three post-it notes with important phone numbers.

'What's all this racket about?' said Lynn, who had ploughed through the hallway and into the office space. She was standing in the doorway like a figurehead, her long dress billowing around her hips.

'We heard about Rhian,' said Rose, completing another

twirl to face Lynn.

'Yes. That,' said Lynn and pointed her face. Her cheeks were smooth and taut, and her skin seemed to be entirely pulled upwards into that bun of hers. 'She's been let go. A stunning fellow came to take her away just a few minutes ago. Really good teeth,' Lynn said. Rose thought she detected admiration behind her smirk. And was that a second row of teeth gleaming in Lynn's mouth? No, she was imagining it; people didn't just turn into sharks.

Rose's mind was buzzing, mentally drafting the text she longed to send to her friends about this, knowing it would be too much to share, too much backstory to explain. She already had plans to meet Hanna for a drink after work that day, but she couldn't bring herself to even introduce her to the present situation. So she waited for Lynn to leave the room. At least she could talk to her colleagues about it, which was almost as good as talking to her real friends.

'It wasn't a real shark, was it, Jim?' Rose said as she half-walked, half-paddled over to his desk. He was hard at work again, typing away. He only looked up at her very reluctantly, shrugged, and went back to staring at his screen.

'Do you mind? I'm kind of in the middle… working on a tough client, this Promise has got to go out before 5 o'clock… going to the printers.'

Yeah, whatever, thought Rose.

'Of course. Sorry,' she said. Robert pulled a face at her as she made her way back to the door.

'Was it a real shark, then?' he asked.

'Maybe Trevor knows something,' suggested Kerry.

Rose led the small party out into the hallway. Opening and closing doors was getting increasingly difficult, as you had to move a whole wedge of water, sending a tidal ripple crashing against the hallway and all its doors.

More algae had started to sprout where the water lapped at the wallpaper, bits of it were beginning to go wavy and peel off. Little specks of plankton were floating in the water, and while it wasn't dirty per se, parts of it had gone slightly cloudy, so you couldn't really see your feet anymore when you walked along. This was great for Rose, who finally felt like she might be able to take off her shoes and socks, because nobody would be able to see her monkey toes anymore.

As the little congregation drifted past the open door to Siobhan's and Rose's office, they spotted Siobhan back at her desk, typing away on the computer. Sterlington was in a corner, on a floating cushion, looking distraught.

'Hey, did you hear about Rhian?' Rose said, leaning against the door frame and splashing about in the water with both hands.

'Yeah,' said Siobhan looking down at her keyboard. The typing continued.

'Actually,' she added and turned to look at Rose. She continued typing. It was like her hands were operating separately from her body.

'Actually, the shark came in here looking for you first.'

Rose suddenly found herself agreeing with Kerry. The water around her felt freezing.

Robert and Kerry, who had trailed after Rose, stopped behind her and leaned closer. She could feel their ears pricking up.

'Why?'

'I don't know. But you know what happened to Rhian.'

'Shit.'

Siobhan kept looking at Rose, and there was blame in her eyes. If Siobhan was Superman, it would've been a laser beam.

Rose's trousers had stuck to her legs all day, but now they felt clammy, like she could feel the fabric sticking to her calves, feel the wetness getting at her skin, soaking the bottom of her shirt, travelling upwards on the threads of her black blouse. Her cuffs and sleeves were wet too, blacker than the rest of her shirt, and they dripped on her face when she wiped a loose strand of hair out of her eyes.

Shit.

Her mind rattled through the past few days. She felt relieved, but in a weird way, because she hadn't known that she was in any danger at all, and she was only finding out now that the danger had passed. Or had it? Would he come back?

'Did he say he'd come back for me?' she said.

Siobhan licked her lips. 'He didn't say anything. He just moved on to the big office.'

'I'll come back for you,' whispered Robert in a creepy, gravelly voice, and Kerry giggled.

It wasn't funny to Rose.

She chuckled, but everything about it was fake. She felt like she might cry.

'Let's talk to Trevor,' she suggested, and turned back around. Siobhan went back to her computer. Sterlington whined in the corner, his blond fur sticking up on his head.

Trevor couldn't tell them anything of any substance. He said that yes, someone had come in earlier, but he couldn't be sure who it was because he was so involved in a game of Bejewelled against his all-time arch-enemy Albert264 from Hungary. Kerry and Robert suggested he might not be doing his job, since his job description clearly stated that he was meant to greet people and direct them to the right office. He insisted that no, actually, his job was to man the front desk, and he was still manning the desk while he was rearranging gems on a screen.

Rose said nothing.

The shark had asked for her.

Rose's friend Hanna was waiting outside for her after work. She had draped herself glamorously over a bench outside Tollcross Mansion. Rose didn't like that Hanna was picking her up, she wished they had just arranged to meet at the pub. She glanced up at the fourth floor, checking the windows for any sign of unusual happenings. But the water wasn't that high yet, it had only splashed up to the window sills occasionally. Her secret was safe, for now. Before meeting Hanna, she had changed from wet office-wear to dry office-wear in one of the ground floor bathrooms, stashing away the soaking clothes into a secure double-bagging situation at the bottom of her vast handbag which, itself, had been wrapped in a protective layer of cling film all day.

'Hey!' said Hanna, looking up from her phone.

'You look lovely!'

'Thanks!' she got up and took a bow. The wind ballooned

her dress out around her.

'How's your building?'

'It's fine,' said Hanna, and smiled.

Then she talked about her work. Her words were reassuring and regular and trickled into Rose's ears like soothing herbal ear oil, as if Rose's predicament had been due to an ear infection and not a shark situation. But Rose couldn't concentrate. Her thoughts still ticked away at the word she couldn't let go of:

Shark.

They had a drink.

'If I get chips, will you have some?' said Rose on the way to the bar. The pub was crowded with after-office chatter.

'Yes please,' said Hanna. She leaned back on the wooden bench, her hair touching the window behind her, wiping a spot of it clean from the condensation that had built up.

When she returned with the drinks and their table number on a little wooden stick, Hanna was holding Rose's phone.

'It won't stop ringing. You're popular.'

Rose put down the two pints. The vibration was urgent and consistent, and when Rose turned the phone over, the ID declared that 'Siobhan Work' was calling her, and had done so a few times already, as indicated by the accusatory red phone symbol in the upper left-hand corner of the screen.

'Sorry,' said Rose. She took the phone and pushed the drinks across the table. Hanna leaned in and sucked the foam off one of the beers, then started drawing in the beer sweat on the outside of the glass.

'It's cool. If the chips arrive before you're back I'll eat them.'

'That's fair. I won't be long.'

Rose stepped outside to take the call. The air was nice and dry after the tropical humidity of the pub. She answered the phone quickly while it was still vibrating.

'Yes?'

'Hi there, Rosie. It's Siobhan,' Rose felt cold inside. Siobhan had never called her Rosie before. No-one called her Rosie, except for her gran. Rosie? Why?

'Hi!' she said, a bit uneasily. She racked her brain. Had she forgotten anything in the office?

'Just checking you're okay, really. Sorry, had a feeling you were a bit shocked by the whole thing.'

They hadn't had a proper chat since the shark thing had happened, or had failed to happen, since it hadn't really happened. Or rather, it *had* happened but not to Rose. It had happened to Rhian, but it was meant to have happened to Rose. Perhaps she was feeling a bit tipsy.

'Aw, that's nice!' said Rose.

She couldn't think of any other words.

She tried to imagine where Siobhan was calling her from.

There were cars in the background, so she was probably outside. Did she step out of a bar to make a phone call, too? Or was her window open in her flat? Maybe Sterlington sat outside in the garden while she did the washing up with an open window. An open window by which she could now stand and make a weird phone call to her colleague, overstepping all boundaries that had previously existed between them.

She still hadn't followed up her comment with anything. Siobhan was breathing.

'Yeah! No, I'm fine. But thanks!'

There was still silence, and breathing, and cars.

'How are you?' said Rose, after another break.

'I'm fine. Are you busy?'

'Sort of,' said Rose.

It was like Siobhan was waiting to say something.

Rose could hear her heartbeat in her eardrums. Siobhan had never called her before. How did she even have her number? And why would she call and not text?

'Right. I thought maybe you wanted to get a drink or something? I feel bad about earlier, we weren't exactly nice about the whole thing. I think everyone's just a bit on edge.'

'Yeah, sure, I mean, I guess we could go for a drink. When are you free? Friday?'

'I was more thinking we could go with the people from the office.'

Oh fuck, Rose, this is so embarrassing.

Rose tried to picture what Siobhan's drink of choice might be, maybe a rosé or an Aperol spritz. She glanced back at Hanna in the pub. Siobhan had never asked her to go for a drink before. She wanted to say yes, let's go right now, wanted to talk to someone about the shark situation, but she also couldn't think of a way to leave that wouldn't offend Hanna.

'Right. Look, I don't want to keep you. Just... don't be scared of him. He might not come back. They might have what they want.'

'What do you mean?' Rose turned around, someone

had emerged from the pub and lit a cigarette. She walked a few more steps out onto the pavement.

She could see Hanna's head leaning against the window from the inside of the bar.

'I'm just saying, they sacked somebody. He probably won't be back for you.'

'Thanks?' said Rose.

Siobhan still sounded like she was holding back. Like she had something hidden behind her back and was waiting to pull it out and push it into Rose's face. Not a bunch of flowers, either. A file with Rose's name on it, perhaps. Something was weird.

'I'm sorry about earlier.'

'Yeah. Thanks.'

'You're busy. I'll see you tomorrow,' Siobhan must've sensed the lack of belief in Rose's voice.

'Sorry. Yeah. I appreciate it, Siobhan. Bye' said Rose, and hung up.

It was so weird.

Why would Siobhan call her?

And with so much *nothing* to say, too?

God. Now she had to walk back to the pub. She'd have to say something to Hanna. She felt like she was leading a very boring double life: one where she worked in an office, and another where she worked in a very similar, slightly flooded office, which was otherwise exactly the same.

She entered the bar and walked through the air, thick with ale, and explained to Hanna that Siobhan had forgotten her key card and she'd wanted to check that Rose would be in to let her into the building the next morning. As she talked about it, she got so worked up she started believing it herself. It was much more believable, after all, than the shark business.

WEDNESDAY

It turned out that the imaginary Siobhan key-card dilemma was completely irrelevant the next day because all of Floor 4 was congregated in the lobby, including Siobhan and Rose. Rose and her colleagues were waiting there, buzzing, because Lynn was going to tell them exactly what was going to happen.

'Rhian was only the first one. You'll see,' said Jim.

Lynn appeared in a wetsuit cut to look like a three-piece office costume, complete with cardigan and little collared blouse. Rose felt like she might be sick. The material was too thick and the collar, cut to be dainty and round, stuck out from her throat like bony gills.

'As you'll no doubt be aware, there is a flooding situation occurring on our floor,' said Lynn in a polite sing-song. Her hair was slickly and firmly in place. Rose suspected that she had combed gelatine through it, like how synchronised swimmers did their hair.

'There is absolutely no need for concern, as I have said many times,' Lynn smiled around the group, her face imitating warmth. It looked like she was physically repulsed by her own facial expression, like her body was rejecting the position her lips had been pulled into.

'There are some new regulations, however. We have provided weight belts for our office staff, so nobody's floating around in the office or such nonsense,' she said and chuckled into the crowd. Her laugh was met by many blank stares and a few half-hearted sharp breaths through the nose that indicated that the attempt at a joke had at least been acknowledged.

'What about ...drowning?' said Siobhan into Rose's ear. Rose shrugged. The back of her neck prickled.

'Secondly, we will be installing some lockers here in the lobby, as well as repurposing some of the restrooms into changing facilities.'

Siobhan looked at Rose, and she could feel the gaze poking her in the back of her head, but she didn't turn around. She was feeling too warm, too blushy to react.

Lockers.

'And that's it! There is absolutely no need to worry. All will be well. It is a safe environment,' Lynn nodded.

Lynn's need to stress the safety of it all so many times made Rose suspect the exact opposite.

'You didn't think we'd just abandon you!' Lynn said. Rose noticed the first person plural. 'They couldn't just abandon us,' Lynn corrected. But Rose had heard.

Was Lynn up for a promotion?

'Anyway, Evan will be upstairs to explain everything in full,' Lynn concluded.

They all piled into the lift. Well, not piled. They walked in like normal people and when there was not enough room to stand anymore they stood back and the doors closed and the people left in the lobby waited for the lift to return. Rose had used her pointy elbows to ensure she would be one of the first people up on the fourth floor. She had to see this.

The water was up to Rose's chest.

There was a shark waiting with his arms full of weight belts. He was wearing a suit.

His arms were normal human arms.

He appeared to have normal human legs.

'Welcome to Floor 4! The experiment begins here!' he said. Lynn giggled and turned to stand next to him. He quickly put a weight belt round her so she couldn't swim about closer to the ceiling, like the rest of the lift load of people had just started to do.

'Over here, you slackers!' the shark laughed again. 'Let's get you all kitted out. We've spared no expense!'

Rose looked down at the shark's face. It was unmoving and pointing upwards, with holes for ears, jagged gills, and a sharp edge where it connected to his suited shoulders.

Underneath its pointy chin it had two small holes, where human eyes peeked into the room.

'Brilliant! Get over here,' he said, his voice muffled. He walked closer and pulled on Rose's arm. His human hand was wrapped around her elbow, and soon she was floating in front of him, her eyes level with the bottom of the shark head, where it met the neat double Windsor of a blue paisley tie. Lynn had wobbled closer, her weird round collar flapping up and down slowly, and she half-hugged Rose from behind to hold her down while the shark put Rose's weight belt on around her waist. She immediately felt more grounded, but also like she wanted Lynn to let go of her shoulders, and Evan to take off that stupid shark head.

With the water to her chest and the belt pulling her down, Rose didn't feel so comfortable anymore.

'What's with the face, Mr Humperdink?' she asked.

'I thought it would build morale, since the fourth floor is now such a lively aquarium!' he said, and chuckled.

Fucking sharkface.

'Hah!' Rose brought herself to say. It might have sounded like a laugh to someone who really wanted to believe that she was laughing. Someone like Evan. Even through the mask Rose could see that he was looking smug and very pleased with himself indeed.

'Who's next?' he boomed out to the people lined up where the wall met the ceiling. The next lift load of people were on their way, and so far only three out of seven people in the office were standing upright on the ground. The rest were having a nice ring-a-rosie on the water's surface.

It was going to be a long day.

Rose watched Lynn walk to her corner office door, when she opened the door, a swarm of tiny fish came flying around her. They were more scared of her than she was scared of them, although she appeared to be scared enough, judging from her high-pitched yelp. Lynn's fish tank had finally been submerged in the surrounding water, and all her little pets had escaped. Well, not all of them.

Rose walked closer. As she reached Lynn's corner office door, she spotted a small octopus sitting in the fish tank. She had never noticed it before. It was purple and had pink suckers which were stuck to the glass walls - one of its arms was slung casually over the rim of the tank.

All of Lynn's office furniture was bolted to the ground. The water distorted everything, so it looked like Lynn's chair was wonky and merging into her desk.

Lynn backed away from her office to get help, and Rose saw her eyes dart back and forth from one fish to the next, like she was looking for something. Maybe she was counting them. Trust Lynn to count the fish. She was probably taking stock. Filing a damage report. Who knows.

The colourful cloud of them dispersed around the staff of Floor 4, who were still bobbing near the lift and lining up with a remarkable amount of discipline to be fitted for a weight belt by a man wearing a shark face on his head.

Rose stood in the doorway looking about. It really wasn't that big an office. Lynn's desk supplies had all been nailed down too, including the stapler and the tin for her pens. The pens themselves were floating at the surface, a sharpie chasing a fountain pen's lonely lid down the current Lynn had created when she opened the door. The window looked like it was straining against the pressure, but it was holding up okay. There was a square sheet of plastic stuck to its frame with big blobs of hot glue, and the curtains made very pretty ripples of dark blue and white lace. Instead of hanging down, they floated horizontally at chest height.

Lynn was the only person who had curtains in her office.

No one else spent enough time at Tollcross Mansion to want, or even notice, that sort of embellishment around their windows, not when most of their time was spent trying not to stare outside at the people walking around in the sunshine.

Lynn's office phone was standing high in the water with the upended receiver stretching its curly cord, like some sort of weird plant. Rose checked back on the octopus. It was still inside the tank, although the inside and the outside of the tank had become similar things. Even the little plastic castle that had adorned the back wall of the tank had floated upwards and was now happily rocking above the octopus's head like a cheerful iceberg. Rose remembered seeing the castle during a meeting in Lynn's office, on a foggy day in May. The buildings outside had seemed so far away, hidden behind a wall of fog, and it was funny to her that the one clear architectural shape in her entire vicinity was a green plastic castle at the back of an unnecessary fish tank.

'Are you looking for something?' said Lynn, who had crept up behind Rose. Even for Lynn, her tone was rude. Rose could only imagine what had made her this upset: maybe it was the same thing that was on everyone else's mind, which was, she guessed, how the hell they would continue working in an environment like this.

'We've got a meeting at two. See you then,' said Lynn, and walked closely behind Rose until she had effectively pushed her out of the office using Rose's need for personal space as a weapon.

'Excuse me,' said Rose, pushing through the crowd that was still gathered in the hallway. Now everyone was wearing their belts over their clothes. Kerry, who was quite short, looked panicked: the water reached her shoulders. Rose was headed for the toilet. It was still a normal trip to take, because it hadn't quite sunk in that they were useless.

She locked herself in a cubicle, took a deep breath, and sat down on the toilet lid. She put her hands in her wet cloud of hair. Now that everything was wet, everything also seemed sort of dry. That didn't make any sense to Rose, but then, neither did anything else. She stood back up for breath, then leaned against the cubicle wall.

Rose thought about washing her face to clear her perspective, or lighting a secret cigarette, but neither seemed like viable options. So she just stood for a while, and let her wet hair make little concentric circles where it dripped onto the water.

She wondered, for the first time, if there was anything in the water that could harm her. Surely, if they were all poisoned and floating with their bellies upwards, their productivity would sink considerably. Or, Rose thought, maybe there wouldn't be a difference. She had always secretly suspected that her work at MoneyTownCashGrowth was meaningless. She had her clients and she sold them things, but none of it actually meant anything. The Bonds and Promises were just words on a page.

'Oh shit shit shit shit shit,' someone came into the ladies' room and cursed.

The swearing was followed by loud sobbing, and panicked gasps that sounded muffled.

Rose closed her eyes and rubbed at them, then undid the latch on her cubicle door to check who had come into her secret sanctuary.

It was Siobhan. Her hair was a long question mark

trailing behind her. She fanned her face with one hand and held a paper bag to her mouth and nose with the other, breathing frantically into it. Her head was tilted backwards. When she saw Rose, her face pulled into a grimace of embarrassment and relief. It had the pulled-up eyebrows of someone who's happy to see another person, the strained jaw muscles of someone who wished that they hadn't been seen, and the flared nostrils of someone thinking they were drowning.

'You're fine! Just breathe normally! Look, you're going to run out of oxygen that way,' said Rose, but it all came out like jumbled blabbering. She tried again, closer to Siobhan's ear.

'Just breathe,' she said again, and pulled the soggy bag from Siobhan's grip as gently as she could. Siobhan puffed her cheeks, and opened her eyes really really wide, so there was more white than blue. It looked scary.

Rose threw the bag in the general direction of the rubbish bin.

The door opened again, and behind Siobhan's puffed cheeks Rose could see a flash of purple, and the door slammed shut again. Whatever. She'd deal with it later. For now, she had to gently poke Siobhan in both of her cheeks with her pointed fingers.

'Blergh,' spluttered Siobhan. She was very white in the face, whiter than normal, and her breaths were slow and short.

'Slowly. There you go. Another deep breath. In and out.'

'There's not enough,' said Siobhan. Rose thought she might cry.

Siobhan was clinging to the tiles on the wall. Her hand

slipped, and she set off the hand drier. Its warm air gently pushed both of the women closer to the stalls, drifting along the floor like children on a frozen river.

The purple thing was on the floor. It was the octopus that had made its way here from Lynn's office. Rose's initial thought was that it, too, had felt that everything was just a bit much out there and wanted a moment of peace and quiet. She wasn't in the mood for apologies, but if she had been, she might have let the octopus know that they'd be right out and then it could have the ladies room to itself.

The octopus slid underneath one of the stall doors and disappeared there.

'Look at me. Look at me,' said Rose, her hand on Siobhan's shoulder.

Siobhan's eyes were bloodshot. She really didn't look well.

'Okay,' said Siobhan.

'In. Out,' said Rose, and then exaggerated her own breaths.

Siobhan copied her.

'There's not enough air in here,' she explained, after two more regular breaths.

'I know it seems that way. But it's fine,' said Rose, and noticed a smear of algae across the white ceramic sinks.

After a short pause and more breathing, Rose said, 'Where's Sterlie?' She thought she'd try out a nickname. Immediately, she sensed that she had overstepped a line.

'Sterlington?' said Siobhan, and the name had never sounded quite that long. It was as though it came crawling out of her mouth like a really long worm. 'He's good. I left him downstairs. They did say he'd be fine and he'd be allowed to swim and everything, but he wasn't happy when the water was up to here,' said Siobhan, indicating her waist, 'so I imagined he'd be pretty livid if he could see the situation as it is now.'

Rose, herself, had rarely seen Sterlington express any sort of negative emotion. She couldn't fathom that he'd ever be livid about anything. The most upset she had seen him was the first day of the flood; since then, he'd been remarkably well adjusted.

'Right. Well, I hope you're okay.'

'I think I will be.'

Siobhan turned to look at herself in the mirror that stretched all along one side of the bathroom.

'Your hair's fine. Everyone's looks like this now,' said Rose and patted her own wet tangle of hair. She grabbed a hair tie that was snug around her wrist, and pulled it around the top third of her hair. Now she looked like she had a drooping fountain emerging from the top of her head, too wet to stand upright and look cheerful.

'You go on out there. I think I'll take another minute or two,' said Siobhan, and headed for the octopus's stall. 'Thank you,' she said. Rose smiled.

They could work it out amongst themselves, thought Rose, and left the bathroom. Just before she closed the door, she called in a quick reminder about the meeting at two, although she figured that Siobhan already knew about it and the octopus probably cared very little.

The hall was completely changed. The commotion had resolved itself, and the only person left out there was Trevor, sitting at his desk like everything was normal. He wore a long snorkel and goggles.

'Alright?' said Trevor, barely glancing up at Rose.

It came out like they were in a bathtub together, playing a game of 'guess which song I'm singing under water'. The snorkel distorted his voice into a thin whine.

'Yeah, good, thanks. See you later on!' As she walked past, she saw that he was rearranging jewels on a screen, which promptly disappeared in the right combination.

Everything as usual, then.

Rose walked to her office, where both her phone and Siobhan's were now also standing up on their cords like seaweed. Sterlington's drifting armchair was blocking the view out of the window. Other than that, everything was either attached to the desks or spread peacefully in the corners of the room, collecting a subtle layer of bright-green algae.

When she closed the door, she saw two pairs of goggles and snorkels hanging on the coat hooks, labelled S and R. She took hers, and put it on. She was angry, but not angry enough to drown herself. She wouldn't give Evan the satisfaction.

She envisioned just what kind of email she would send to him. The taste of rubber and disinfectant in her mouth mingled with spit and rage.

What *do* you say to a man who dresses up as a shark in a suit? She dipped under water and sat down in her swivel chair and got to work.

From: relli@moneytowncashgrowth.co.uk
To: ehump@moneytowncashgrowth.co.uk
Subject: Today

```
Dear Mr Humperdink,

So you think it's super funny that
we're all under water? Why don't you
try to ACTUALLY DO ANY WORK when
you're SUBMERGED IN WATER? Wanker.
```

She breathed in and out. The corners of her lips were straining against the unfamiliar shape of the mouthpiece.

```
Dear Mr Humperdink,

I am glad you think the situation is
funny. HOWEVER, it is not that funny
for me and all my colleagues working
here on Floor 4.
```

The cursor blinked on and off after that sentence. Rose stared at it. She exhaled through her nose in frustration and made her goggles fog up.

Rose thought of her previous emails. She'd always scrambled for requests. What could she ask for?

```
Dear Mr Humperdink,

Kindly stop being such a massive
tool.

Best wishes,
Rose.
Floor 4.
Not amused.
```

No, that wasn't a reasonable request. And besides, Evan

was way too pleased with himself to agree to it. Rose thought of his eyes behind the shark chin. He thought he was so funny.

```
Dear Mr Humperdink,

I just wanted to let you know
that your callous disregard for
the turmoil of Floor 4 is not
appreciated.
I appreciate-
I think-

I can understand that you may have
thought that your costume would have
helped raise the spirits in the
office, but I can assure you that it
has done the exact opposite.
I would appreciate-
I would hope that in consideration
for the feelings of staff on Floor
4 you will refrain from wearing the
aforementioned costume during our
meeting this afternoon.

Kind regards,

Rose.
```

She sent it.

She pushed her chair back, and it slid through the water slowly.

Siobhan entered the office. She looked like she had fresh make-up on, special grade 'Floor 4' waterproof mascara and meticulously combed eyebrows.

'I just emailed Evan. Fucking sharkface.' She hated her voice through the plastic tube, so she stood up, spat out her mouthpiece, and repeated herself.

'I know! What was that all about?,' said Siobhan, and walked to the window to rest her hand on the armchair that was floating there.

'The worst thing is, I think he thought he was being funny. And he had the nerve to tell me he was building *morale*,' Rose said. Morale. What a dick.

'What did you write?'

'I told him not to wear the face to the meeting, or else,' said Rose.

'Or else what?' said Siobhan as she walked back to the door.

'I didn't say.'

'Oh. Good one,' she gave Rose a small wink.

She plucked her underwater gear from the coat hooks, sat down at her desk, and started typing. It really was a normal day. Rose crouched down to stick her face into the water to look at the screen and closed her email programme, when she figured Evan wouldn't respond. Then she dialled a number on the phone and reeled her phone receiver in to call her first client of the day.

'Yes, Mrs Gradlaw, it's good to finally speak to you. I'm calling because I've been referred by your bridge partner, Professor Jane Fair? Oh! Lovely!' She was expecting the call, and really eager to make a purchase. The first positive surprise of the day.

It was closely followed by another surprise: a response to her email. Rose squinted to read it on her screen through the ripples of the water.

From: ehump@moneytowncashgrowth.co.uk
To: relli@moneytowncashgrowth.co.uk
Subject: Re: Today

Dear Ms Ellis,

Good to hear from you, sorry I didn't
get back to you sooner, have been
absolutely swamped (!) with emails.
Really treading water here (!). I
could go on.
Anyway, sorry to hear you feel that
way about the costume. Everyone else
really seemed to like it, so it will
certainly be making an appearance
later. Hope you won't mind.

See you there,

It'd be lovely to have a chat
sometime,

Evan Humperdink
Not Actually A Shark

MoneyTownCashGrowth
Bonds | Promises | Trust

'Sorry, what was that?' Rose had completely missed what
Mrs Gradlaw had said on the phone for the past minute.
Never mind that the water made the already shabby line
even more crackly, but the email had distracted her to
such a degree that she couldn't be sure she hadn't just

missed a vital and intimate account of Mrs Gradlaw's financial history.

'No, I'm here. Great. I will send you your first package over as soon as you give me your details. Fabulous.'

What a dick.

Not Mrs Gradlaw. She seemed fine.

As soon as Rose had hung up the phone, she picked it back up again. She got through to Madison's secretary, because Madison had a secretary, and made sure that Madison would call her back immediately.

Fucking sharkface.

She called Hanna, who picked up the phone immediately, because she didn't have a secretary who could've done it for her.

'Yes?'

'Want to have lunch later? The Turkish place?'

'I'm down in Gorgie, on a building site.'

'Oh, that's exciting!'

'Yeah,' she exhaled loudly. Rose waited. Then Hanna said, 'I can be there at 12.'

Madison's secretary called Rose back. She tried to ignore Siobhan's glances, which betrayed jealousy and annoyance and irritation and a number of other sub-emotions in between, like hunger and sadness and possibly the memory of choking in the bathroom earlier.

'Yes, she can make it. Send me the address and we'll have a car take her there,' said the secretary. His voice was sugar-coated.

Rose imagined that he had a tiny shiny office to himself, next to Madison's, with nothing but a wireless telephone and an impressive collection of Texan cacti. And no in-house swimming pool you're only allowed to walk in. None of that.

'The meeting's in a few hours, you know,' said Siobhan, snorkel-voiced, without looking up from her computer.

'Yeah. I might not go,' said Rose. She didn't think Siobhan had heard her through the water, but that was okay. She could go to lunch with some friends. Office policy could forbid her from swimming, but lunch was still allowed, as far as she knew.

She busied herself with rearranging the pages on a soaking-wet Promise filed near her stapler, which she placed under a rock that was growing an impressive head of moss and other tendrils. She didn't think twice about it. Her office was a fish tank now.

'Or I might. Who knows,' she said, and smiled at Siobhan.

It was barely 10am, so Rose sat down and wrote up Mrs Gradlaw's Promise as carefully as she could. Her hands were shaking. Evan was such a dick. With every punch of a key, she felt her rage piling and piling on top of itself, until she felt ready to explode.

Siobhan made another couple of calls, and then went downstairs to take an oxygen break, as she called it. Rose imagined her standing there in the lobby, leaning against the revolving door, breathing in the air that wasn't limited by a thick layer of water.

Rose hoped Siobhan was okay. When she came back into the office, she looked a bit less pale, and a bit more sure of herself as she pulled on her new face gear again and breathed steadily through the snorkel. It was perfectly vertical in the water as she sat at her desk. Rose was very impressed with how calm she was now. Rose also felt a bit of smugness, a trace of pride, like maybe she had something to do with Siobhan's new confidence in the water.

It was 11:30. Rose gathered her things and left. She breezed past Trevor, who was sticky-taping his shiny reception bell to the desk. The sticky tape wouldn't last, but he would find that out for himself. There was no need to be patronising.

'Morning tea?' he asked. 'Bring us a scone!'

'Maybe!' she said, waving as she stepped onto the lift. The floor panel had been removed since she was last on it, leaving only a terrifying grid of metal to stand on. The water that had spilled into the lift drained through it at an alarming rate, and the water in the reception area was now a tiny bit lower. Wherever it was coming from, it would surely fill back up. They had a level to maintain. This was a business, after all.

There was a special kind of wetness one acquired when hanging out in a wet environment all day. A wetness that didn't change, that just reached saturation point and stayed there. It was different to the wetness of those who only visited Floor 4 and went back into their own dry offices afterwards. Their wetness only drenched their hair and clothes, but didn't sink skin deep, didn't make you feel like your eyeballs were wetter than usual, like the backs of your ears were more closely scrubbed than they had been in years.

Walking through the lobby, Rose left a trail of puddles behind. She felt like a person whose car had just run off the road and into a river, who had somehow got out of it in one piece and was now walking to the nearest village, a steady pair of wet footsteps following them wherever they went. She wondered whether she'd grow webs in between her fingers and toes.

It was a bright morning that was slowly turning into a hot day. Her hair in a childish fountain, she was sure the drenched clothes were actually improving her appearance. She walked up the little hill and turned to the left, to where the Kapadokya was. She hadn't gone there for lunch since the flood had started, but they'd have to see her like this eventually. Or not, she thought, if they got lockers, like Evan had suggested. Good idea, Evan. Lockers. Wanker.

The Kapadokya had tables and chairs set up outside for days like today, and, one would assume, for workers from offices that had been put under water. The wicker chairs were comfortably holey and let enough water seep out of her clothes to make her think she wasn't just leaving a damp spot behind. At least the chair and her clothes were working together.

Hanna and Madison arrived almost at the same time. Hanna's wrinkled clothes and film of perspiration on her upper lip suggested a cramped bus-ride from Gorgie, and Madison's goose bumps on her neck told Rose that her company's car was heavily air-conditioned.

'This is nice!' said Madison, which meant something like, 'Why are we all here?'

'Three raki, please,' said Rose, the dripping hostess, to the fifteen-year-old waiter who had just appeared from inside the restaurant. His white shirt was big and flopped around his boyish shoulders. His hair was cut into a sort of elegant mullet, a thing that Rose had never believed existed.

'Sure,' he said, looking frightened and also amused. He put down three laminated menus on the table, and walked back inside to get their drinks. Or to complain about the daytime drinking habits of these three very business-like business women. Hanna and Madison sat down.

'What's with the water?' said Hanna.

'Did you not have time to dry your clothes this morning?' said Madison, and Rose felt overcome with a wave of affection for her friend. Of course she would assume Rose owned a tumble dryer. Bless her fancy little heart.

'I fell into a puddle,' said Rose. She sat back in her chair and waited. Neither of her friends questioned what she'd just said. They appeared to just accept that there were very deep, very wet puddles on the way from Tollcross Mansion up to Lauriston Place.

That would be a hazard.

'So, how's the building site?' said Rose. Hanna rested her face in her open palms.

'Hey, are you crying?' said Madison, and patted her friend's shoulder.

'No. It's just very funny,' said Hanna. 'It's a bus shelter.'

'What?' said Rose and Madison. The waiter was at their table again and set down three shiny shot glasses. They looked dangerous.

'I have to take work when I can get it, you know. I *am* working on the new rugby stadium competition for uni, but that's due at the end of the year, so I thought I'd take some other work in the meantime. And they really really needed a bus shelter in Gorgie.'

'But aren't they all the same?' said Rose. Her cardigan's sleeve had made a circle of water on the concrete floor.

'Well!' said Hanna, taking a sip of raki and wincing. 'I am so glad you asked.'

They took the shot together, made three disgusted faces, and listened.

'They have a normative bus shelter plan, yes, but some areas require different things. This one, for example, is red.'

'Okay,' said Madison and nodded. Her wrinkled forehead made her look very intense. She was probably taking mental notes, just in case bus shelters ever came up in her job.

'And it needs to have round edges, because it's close to a school.'

Rose stifled a yawn.

'Oh, I'm sorry, is this boring to you? Because it's a fucking delight for me, you know,' said Hanna, and licked the semi-circle of leftover liquor from her lips.

There was a moment of silence.

Then laughter.

Hanna started it, to let the other two know it was okay.

'That's ridiculous,' said Rose, and wiped a giggle tear from her cheek.

'You think that's ridiculous? Let me tell you, the things that are going on in the management at MoneyGrowthTownCash, they would blow your mind,' Madison lowered her voice. Rose and Hanna shared a look of surprise; Madison didn't usually complain about her work. Or talk about it. At all.

Rose and Hanna held their breath, and when holding their breath became too exhausting they made sure their breathing was quiet, so as to not scare away the delicate deer that was Madison's Sharing Moment.

'They have us actually licking envelopes. Can you believe it? We get things printed professionally, but... I need another drink.'

Madison stepped into the restaurant and emerged a minute later with a bottle of white wine, the waiter following with a tray of glasses.

'Is that ok? Faster than having to order rounds. So. We have our Apology Bonds printed on professional paper and put into professional envelopes by these printing professionals,' she poured three generous measures, 'but someone decided it was too expensive to pay for the self-adhesive envelopes, so yesterday we all stayed late *literally licking paper*.'

The laughter continued, albeit quietly, because Hanna and Rose were still afraid Madison might stop sharing.

'And don't get me started about my boss,' said Madison.

Rose didn't know that Madison even had a boss.

It seemed to be new information for Hanna, too.

'I swear to God he probably doesn't even know what an Apology Bond is! They're only the things his whole bloody business is built on!'

The three of them laughed again, each with their own embarrassed question about what Bonds really were, and a lingering uncertainty about whether it mattered.

'And I looked up my pension age the other day. Did you know I have to keep contributing for another thirty-seven years? Thirty-seven! That's more than what I've already been alive for!' said Madison. She scrunched up her nose a little bit because the last sentence had come out so weird and ungrammatical, but her friends nodded with understanding.

'I mean, right now it says I'm only eligible for, like, 50 pounds of pension a week! I can't live off that! And I have to keep working until 2055. That's ages away. That's, oh wow, that's the second half of this century.'

A sudden understanding of where they were in time and space settled over the small table outside the Turkish restaurant. It went away again after a blink, but for a second, all three of them had felt very small and infinitely big at the same time.

After another deep sip of wine, they ordered food.

But Rose couldn't wait for it to arrive. She had to say it now.

'Look. I didn't really fall into a puddle,' she said. The other two made appropriately surprised noises. And suddenly she didn't want to do it anymore. Her predicament was clearly the best, and she didn't want to show up her friends for having mildly more boring work stories.

'Um, Hanna, hypothetically, I mean, what do you think would happen if an entire floor of a building was filled with water? Like, from an architectural point of view. Asking for a friend.' There was another spell of tense silence. A tray of olives and fish covered in bubbling cheese approached the table, carried on the strong forearm of the restaurant's proprietor.

'Ladies!' he said, and set it down.

There was polite humming and the moving about of

chairs, but the silence returned like a yo-yo.

'Hypothetically, I think it should be fine. I think water weighs the same as air, so if you think about it it's really already filled with air, so it shouldn't change anything structurally...' said Hanna, and Rose loved her in that moment, because not only was what she was saying factually inaccurate, but she was actually pretending to believe that Rose's situation was hypothetical.

'Oh my God have they filled you up with water?' said Madison through a mouthful of olives.

Rose looked down at her soaking wet trousers and the puddle under her chair. There was no use in hiding it. She was a piece of evidence.

'They did that to an office in Birmingham, you know. It's some management fad, I think. They tried sand, down in Swansea, but it didn't increase productivity at *all*,' added Madison.

'Of course it wouldn't!' said Hanna. Rose felt a rush of protectiveness as she realised Hanna hadn't had to deal with this kind of corporate bullshit since she left MoneyTownCashGrowth.

'I didn't know it wasn't just us,' said Rose.

'Oh, yeah. They've been introducing it everywhere. They've had mixed results, but apparently not enough failures to get them to stop. It's just a craze. It'll end.'

'I hope so! Are you okay? What's it like in there?' said Hanna.

Rose ate a slice of hot cheese with some fish hiding underneath it. Then she explained about the water, and how high it was, and that they had to walk, and about Jim and Siobhan and the octopus. The octopus wasn't really that important but she figured she needed to liven up the depressing subject a little.

'And my boss, or really the CEO's assistant, he's the worst. He's holding a meeting today. Dressed up like a shark.'

'A whole body costume?' said Madison and ate a little vine leaf filled with mint and rice. Some of the rice dropped onto her pristine white blouse. She didn't notice.

'Just the face.'

'Typical. No commitment,' said Hanna.

The teenage waiter came out to check they were enjoying their food. Rose was grateful that Madison took charge of splashing more wine into their glasses. She was quite a heavy-handed pourer, and the bottle already looked rather empty.

'It's great, thanks! Could we get some more bread, please?' said Hanna. The waiter returned promptly with a basket of soft white rolls.

Madison's eyes appeared to grow wider. 'Look at all those carbs!'

'They're beautiful, aren't they?' said Hanna.

Rose was still quiet.

There was nothing weird about saying it out loud. It was a normal thing that happened to other people too. My office got flooded. Big deal! What else is new?

'He sounds like a dick,' said Madison, who tore into a roll and dipped it into the glistening pond of cheese in the terracotta dish.

'Evan? Yeah,' said Rose.

Now she could feel it. They were surely about to say it. You should just quit.

'I'm sure that's not allowed, to mock your employees like that.'

Hanna, and her lack of experience with the Evans of this world! Rose blushed with how much she wished that she, too, still led such a sheltered life.

The fish was spicy, so all of them took a long, deep drink from their glasses.

'Actually, you could probably file a complaint. I'll have my secretary send you over a form,' said Madison, wiping her cheesy fingers on a napkin, and tapping and swiping away on her phone.

'You could get him fired and then you could quit,' said Hanna.

There it was. But it didn't feel patronising at all. It just felt like something a friend would say.

Rose drank some more wine. She said, 'And with the severance money I could… I could fly to Greece, and live on a boat.'

'Yeah!' said Madison.

'Or something else!' said Hanna.

'Anything!' said Rose. She was exhilarated. She was buzzing.

It was her phone.

It was 12:45. They had time.

After the fish and olives and vine leaves, they ate some sticky baklava, the honey and nuts washed down with more of the wine and three small coffees.

And they split the bill, of course. Madison offered to pay but the other two wouldn't have it.

'Another time, yeah?' Madison said, and the other two nodded and meant it.

'Good luck with the bus shelter, Hanna,' Rose said. They all snorted at her beautiful slurred speech. Hanna got a ride from Madison, even though MoneyGrowthTownCash was at the other end of town, and the sheer friendliness of it all made Rose teary-eyed.

'You go in there and you take no one's shit. Not even Evan's,' said Madison.

'None of his shark shit. None of that,' added Hanna.

They waved Rose goodbye, and she stumbled down the hill back to her office.

At a bakery on the corner, she bought an apricot scone for Trevor.

It was 2:05 now. She was late. But it didn't matter. She would march in there and tell Evan what was what, and what she thought of him, and where he could stick that stupid shark smile of his, and then she would book a holiday. And get a haircut. And the hoover needed fixing. But first, the Evan thing!

In the lift she looked at her face. Her outfit had dried in patches, and her cheeks were flushed with tipsiness. But her fountain hair had dried into a nice shape, which gave her some temporary satisfaction as she got ready for the wet embrace of Floor 4.

Rose drifted out of the lift and watched two big gulps of water disappear down the grate in the floor before the doors wooshed shut. The reception desk was empty. Trevor must be at the meeting too, Rose thought. She made sure to hold the paper bag with his scone over her head the whole time, then deposited it on a high shelf above his desk. She hoped he would find it.

With a purposeful breaststroke, a deep breath and

a short dive, she headed towards the conference room, which was just across the hall from her office. The staff of Floor 4 rarely used it, because they rarely had conferences, except for that one time when they met to cast votes on which flavour sandwiches the cafeteria should stock, if they ever got a cafeteria.

It was hard to march into a room when you're swimming, but Rose gave it her best. Her frog leg pushes were strong and sharp, and her arm strokes were round and forceful, shovels for hands. She held on to the top of the door to the conference room and kicked at the door handle, then did a backwards flip into the room, grazing the floor with her knees. She ended up drifting on the surface of the water, a swimming entrance. Her moves couldn't have been any more perfect if she had planned them.

The whole staff of Floor 4, plus a shark-headed Evan, were gathered around the oval conference table. Their long snorkels stuck out from the water. Through the distortion of the ripples, Rose could see that the table's top layer of fake oak was peeling off around the edges, showing the rough MDF underneath. There were pages of an agenda floating around. Some were on the table, held down by rocks. Jim's agenda was weighed down by his gigantic mobile phone, circa 1999, which was encased in a ziplock bag.

'How very good of you to join us, Rose,' said Lynn. She was presiding over the meeting, with Evan sitting to her right, his sharky chin pointing towards the ceiling. Rose could hear Lynn through the plastic tube, but she wasn't sure the others around the table had any idea what she was saying.

'Not a problem, Lynn. It's not actually you I've come to talk to,' Rose said. She wasn't sure she heard her. She swam over to Lynn's end of the table, dipped her face in the water, and repeated her words. They came out distorted and wobbly, but Lynn understood.

'Really?'

'Yes. It's this guy,' Rose pointed at Evan.

'Moi?' he said, placing his hand on his chest in faux disgust at her accusing tone.

Rose motioned Evan to stand up. He waved an apologetic gesture at the others, and followed Rose's lead. He was still wearing the belt, so was standing upright with both his shark and real face peeking out of the water, while Rose paddled away in front of him.

'You! We have been dealing with this stupid flood for two weeks now, and only now does it occur to you to do anything about it?' Rose pounded the surface of the water with her fist, which splashed Evan in his fake face. Rose wasn't sorry at all. 'And when you finally decide to do something to help, you just make a farce of the situation. Tell me, do you think this is a joke? This is what we have to work in, every day! And your stupid belts aren't doing anything to make things better! Tell me, Evan, tell me,' she knew she was overdoing the direct address but the three glasses of wine were running away with her mouth, 'do you think it's easy to walk upright while submerged in water?' She demonstrated this by standing up in the water and doing a quick lap of the conference room, exaggerating her steps, pushing water away from her sides. The overspray went down several people's snorkels, and Siobhan started coughing nervously. This made Rose even more agitated.

'It takes ages! If we could just adapt to what's happening, like normal people, and think about what we're doing, we could be much more efficient!' She pushed herself into a swimming position again, somersaulted, did a little twirl, then dove down on the other side of the table and emerged upright, leaning against a windowsill.

'That's enough, Rose,' said Lynn, but Rose held up a hand.

Siobhan was watching her closely. Her cheeks were flushed, she still looked a little bit shocked, and there was fear in her eyes. The others, too, watched every one of Rose's moves from underneath the surface of the water. At first, it looked like admiration to her, but then she started thinking that the faces of her audience were more like the faces of people who are watching a horrible car crash unfold.

'But none of this matters, you know,' and she lifted her hand to gesture at Evan, or in his general direction. 'You want to meet with me. And I know why. But, you see,' Rose had an idea, 'You can't fire me now! I quit!' and she turned to march out of the room. The same problem presented itself to her again – marching is pretty hard in a room filled with water, so she proceeded to glide, slowly.

'No, you know what, no,' she turned around again, creating a little whirlpool that sucked up some of the loose leaflets from the table. 'You owe me an explanation. And not just me! All of us!' She dug her hands into her sides, folded her arms, unfolded them again, then settled on leaning against the wall in a threatening, I-won't-budge-an-inch sort of stance.

'Rose,' Evan said and turned his shark face towards her, 'I was actually going to offer you Lynn's position, since she'll be leaving us,' a collective gasp through plastic tubes rushed around the room, 'Or, leaving you, I should say, to join me on the seventh floor, as my assistant.'

'Aren't you already assistant to the CEO?' said Robert.

'He is. But we're all expanding and Evan gets to hire an assistant for himself now, and besides, I don't see how it's any of your concern, actually,' said Lynn quickly before Evan could even open his mouth.

'Sorry, can we go back to what you said just then?' said Rose.

'Yes, I was going to ask you for a meeting because I think you'd fit well into Lynn's shoes, as it were,' said Evan and a hollow chuckle emerged out of his shark face.

'Not literally,' said Lynn.

'No, not literally,' said Evan, in agreement.

'Okaybutcouldwereschedule,' said Rose. She felt the need to not be in the situation anymore. She was hot all over, and felt her forehead and her palms sweating despite the fact that she was bobbing up and down in a pool of cool office water.

'Pardon?' said Evan, and Rose could hear the smug smile in his voice.

'Do you think. That. It's possible. For us to reschedule. Please?' said Rose, and with every word she felt she needed to be more careful, so careful that the last word barely emerged at all. 'Please,' she said again.

'Certainly. Now, would you care to join us for the rest of the meeting?'

Siobhan shifted aside, making room for a chair for

Rose.

'Actually, no,' Rose heard herself say, 'I forgot my snorkel. I lost it. And, um, I've got a dental appointment. Now. For the rest of the day. But thanks! Thanks for the offer! And thanks! See you tomorrow,' and she walked to the door, paddling water at her sides.

In the hallway, after she made sure the door was closed, she let out a long sigh. A little yellow fish from Lynn's aquarium came to see her, and together they swam to the lift. The fish must have needed to stay at the office and finish his day at work, but she left as quickly as she could. She dripped water down the grate in the lift, waved goodbye to the girl at the front desk in the lobby, and stepped out into the sunshine.

Rose had that distinct tipsy person's sense of purpose as she hailed a taxi to take her home. She was grateful for the cabbie's offer of a plastic lining for the seat, and changed into her pyjamas as soon as she got home. She left her sopping wet clothes in a pile by the bathroom door, with the honest intention of hanging them up to dry when she got up. And then she took a nap on her sofa, underneath a dry tartan blanket, after she had set an alarm for six o'clock. In her inebriated determination she had settled on taking a train to Dunbar for that evening, to get out onto the waves and clear her head and also work off some of the cheesy calories from her decadent lunch. But mostly the waves. She opened her weather app and checked the swell she was likely to anticipate for Dunbar. It wasn't ideal but it wasn't terrible either.

Rose was comfortably unhungover when she woke up

a few hours later, due mostly to the fact that she was still a little bit tipsy. The kind of tipsy where your knees are shaky, but not too shaky to go surfing. She packed up all her things, lifted her board over her head and marched out into the sunshine of the afternoon. She reckoned she still had about three hours of normal sunlight, and it'd be okay to get home as it set, watching it go down from the train window. Her drunk self might have planned this trip, but her sober self was happy to carry it out.

She slept a little bit more on the train. Her dreams were white and blue, and she felt like she was a bird. Like she was dry, finally, and surrounded by billows of wind, flying free. How good, then, she thought as she woke up, that she'd soon be getting quite wet again.

She waded through the brashy bit of water before the open sea and saw a boat coming into shore. It was a small sailing boat with the word Serenity painted on the side. Rose thought that she'd probably buy a nicer boat with her nice new salary, and name it something more fun. Then she thought that she hadn't even decided whether or not she'd take the job yet. Then she decided to stop thinking and get on with the surfing.

It was a quiet day out at sea, with long, languid waves. She could feel them coming, rolling in from the big wave factory in the ocean.

Rose turned her board horizontally, pointing it along the coast. She clung on, the strap tight around her ankle, and floated for a bit. It was a bright sunny day, and the sun, although lower on the horizon, was still strong. Its light bounced off the waves and made them shine, made them look glossy and solid.

Feeling the alcohol seep out of her pores into the water around her, Rose turned the board again and hugged it with one arm, pushing herself further out with the other. Rose could feel the waves tickling her toes, bubbly almost, or maybe that was a fish touching her feet.

The tight wetsuit made her feel close to the water, but safe, removed from it by a firm layer of rubber. What would she wear to the office the next day? She felt so comfortable in the wetsuit that she dreaded the thought of wearing anything else. No. Don't think about it.

She closed her eyes against the sun, then she felt a wave.

She couldn't see it properly yet, out in the distance, but she felt a good one coming towards her. She'd be ready.

She turned the board, her back to the wave. Its tendrils tickled the backs of her knees, pushed against her back, made the water splash a little faster around her shoulders.

Rose got on the board.

Don't think about the meeting.

She swam, her chest firmly on the board, her toes bent against the bottom of it, feeling every ridge and scrape. She'd have to get some new wax soon. She couldn't finish her thought, her long swimming strokes, flat and fast, became full; her arms a ring, an embrace.

The wave filled up the space underneath her and pushed her up, up, forward, forward, and she was on top of it, and then she pushed again with her left, with her right arm, held on to the sides of the board, pulled her legs forwards and stood up, pushed her knees out, straightened up, her arms at her sides, and she didn't look down, she looked forward.

She was standing up.

Her thighs and her calves made a tense arch, her toes pressed down, and she balanced her weight with her arms, spread out like wings.

She didn't think about the meeting.

The wave carried her. Foam splashed alongside the board.

The sun was behind the houses on the beach, making their edges glow and their shapes look black. Rose felt lifted, carried. The wave wasn't particularly high, but it was big enough, and it carried enough force to lift her and deliver her safely to the shore.

She figured that once was enough.

When she walked through the grassy water and back to dry land, she discovered she was tired.

Sitting on the beach looking out at the glinting sea, she saw the boat again. Serenity. It was just coming in, and a few of the crew had jumped out to help pull it to shore.

'Throw me that rope there, will you?' said one of them. His shorts were rolled up high on his thighs.

'That's not a rope, pal,' said the other man, whose white long-sleeved shirt was tucked firmly into some heavy-duty rubber fishing trousers.

'Looks like a rope to me,' said the other one, catching the object in question in mid-air. It looked like a rope to Rose, too. It also looked like a headache. She closed her eyes against the sun, which was beginning to set behind the approaching boat.

'A rope's only a rope until it's used. That's a line,' said the man in the white shirt.

Rose made a mental note of it, thinking it would be useful if she ever did decide to become a skipper in a yellow waxy coat and a cable-knit jumper.

Although perhaps she wouldn't have to worry about what exactly a rope was when she was sitting on a nice deck chair on a ferry to Corfu, sipping a beer and eating shrimp with her fingers. Other people would know the difference between a rope and a line, and she'd be able to concentrate on not getting sunburn.

THURSDAY

The meeting was first thing the next day. Rose picked a creamy pink skirt made from a very annoying, thick, rubbery fabric, black leggings that ended at her calves, and a bikini top underneath a floaty black blouse. Her shoes were blue, and they were made of rubber, too, the kind that you wore to the beach if you wanted to avoid cutting up your feet on the sharp shells.

She was going to start dressing sensibly for work.

On her way to the office, her mother called.

'Hello, dear,' she said.

Rose made an affirmative sound through a breakfast croissant. It was a buttery, flaky noise, but her mother appeared to understand.

'How are you? I haven't heard from you in ages, I thought I'd check in.'

'I'm good. How are you?' said Rose. Her voice was greasy and it had a smile.

'I'm fine! I'm just fine. Any news?' she said. Rose thought one of her friends might have told her mum something about the meeting, but then she remembered that she hadn't told any of them about it.

'Yes, actually!' Rose said. She wiped her face with a napkin.

'Oh, have you met somebody? When can we meet them?'

'No, Mum. It's a job.'

'But you already have a job! You've got to start thinking about your future, Rose, if you're ever going to give us grandchildren, planning is everything,' and then Rose interrupted.

'I think I'm about to be promoted, Mum, actually,' and her mum, in turn, interrupted her.

'Oh, that's fabulous! And think of how many eligible bachelors work in higher positions at investment banks! What about the CEO, what was his name?'

'You're thinking of the CEO's assistant, Mum. The CEO is a lady.'

'Well, good for her!' said Rose's mother.

Rose said goodbye as quickly as she could. She felt slightly sick.

Rose entered Floor 4; Trevor was at reception. When he saw her come in, he peeked his head out of the water and took off his snorkel to tell her that her meeting would be in her office. There was some refurbishment issue in the conference room. Something about a filter.

Rose swam down the hallway in swift strokes. There was a cast of little sea crabs lingering in front of her door, green and pink. Some of them got stuck in her hair as she floated through them. Her hair was no longer tied into a fountain, but floating around the back of her head spread out like a starfish.

Evan was already sitting in Siobhan's seat when she

swam into her office. Rose noticed a slick otter sitting on Sterlington's chair, which was floating in its old corner by the door.

'Hello,' she said, and stood at her desk. She wasn't going to have an underwater snorkel conversation. 'Is this your pet?'

'No, I thought it was yours,' said Evan, standing up. He wasn't wearing the mask, which was helpful. His coiffed hair was as firm as Lynn's; they must share a pot of gelatine between them, Rose thought.

'Where's Siobhan?'

'I sent her off to help put in the lockers downstairs. It seemed like she had some opinions on where the best placement for them would be.'

'Right.'

'So, you look lovely today,' said Evan, and smiled a smile. He still looked very much like a shark, with dimples for gills.

'What's the job?' said Rose, and smiled back.

'You're forward. I like that. You know, my last girlfriend was a real hammerhead.'

'Would you like me to call HR?' said Rose, and reeled in her phone from its floating wire.

'Sharp. Right. Lynn's job, basically. You'd be managing sales. You've been very proactive with leading this office into a position of adapting to the current wet situation.' He smiled and waved his arm around to indicate the office, splashing the walls in a circular motion. 'Although I take it I haven't been at all helpful with implementing your changes. We've been swamped upstairs too, but, hah, figuratively.'

'Yes,' said Rose.

He'd already made that joke. He was clearly running out of water-related puns, which could only be a good thing.

She also thought that he might have an extra row of teeth behind his current ones, which would be useful if she punched him in the face right now. He'd have spares. But she breathed quietly.

Think of the view.

The curtains would have to go.

'I appreciate the opportunity. What sort of money are we talking?'

'Oh, a good chunk,' said Evan, and handed over the contract. It was a wet lump of paper, but the figure next to the word 'Proposed salary' was very impressive.

'You'd still be reporting to Lynn, but she'd be on a different floor.'

'Okay.'

Rose's thoughts were starting to spin out of control with all the potential that had just presented itself. She'd rope in all the help she could from the new ecosystem that had started to grow.

She hoped her gaze wasn't too vacant; Evan was still laying out the details of the new job. The otter was swimming in circles and grooming its tail.

With Lynn's power, she could implement lots of changes. It could be the best office ever.

She could have a filing cabinet with flat fish holding down important documents, trained to release them at the right command. Little turtles could carry memos from one office to the next. Swordfish could open letters. Electric eels could curl up around the desk lamps.

Rose had already started drafting the first email as sales director in her head. It would be great.

From: relli@moneytowncashgrowth.co.uk
To: All Staff
CC: ehump@moneytowncashgrowth.co.uk
Subject: Animal Training

Dear all,

There will be a training session for the animals held in the conference room on Tuesday. Can you please make sure to have your animals ready? Please find attached a document with the tasks the animals will be required to carry out. We will have a special animal handler on site to ensure compliance with animal welfare regulations. The environment has been tested and deemed appropriate, and there are no carnivores on site, apart from the piranhas in room 4.12, who will replace all shredders on Floor 4. There will be a training session for all human employees directly following the animal training session to fill you in on the new protocol.

Best wishes,
Rose Ellis
Corner Office

'I'll think about it,' said Rose, and looked at the otter. Evan smiled with his teeth. Rose found a pen floating above her desk, and took the cap off.

She didn't need to move to Greece.

She could always continue surfing on the weekends.

The ink made an octopus cloud above the contract.

Acknowledgements

Thank you to my editor Jen Hutchison, and everybody at Speculative Books: Dale McMullen, Sam Small, Jack McMillan. Thank you also to Anna Toffolo for the beautiful cover and Moonshake Designs for the amazing chapter numbers.

For reading various iterations of this story and providing vital guidance and advice, thank you to Jane McKie, Robert Alan Jamieson, Alison Carlyle, Graham Robertson, Russell Jones and Sim Bajwa.

For pointing out the reflection of brilliant blue sky in the windows of a high-rise office building and saying 'it looks like that's flooded with water,' and for making our home a boat, thank you to Natasha Warder. For the title and for cinnamon sugar toast, thank you to Anna Pitt.

For office details, thank you to Chris Price. For surfing details, thank you to Jonny Lewtas. For corporation names, thank you to Oscar Lampe. For boat names, thank you to Phil Power.

Thank you to the Novella Award, specifically Ciarán Hodgers. For their brilliant novellas and co-adventuring, thank you to Jacques Tsiantar and Joma West.

For encouragement, thank you to Matthias Mayer, Layla AlAmmar, Jenny Gray, Celeste Trottier, Peta Freestone,

Julie Fergusson, Claire Askew, Ross McCleary and Heather McDaid.

Thank you to Sasha de Buyl-Pisco, Alice Tarbuck and Dave Coates.

Thank you to Maria Stoian.

Thank you to my family: the Neuwirths and the Collinses.

Thank you to Ardie Collins, for everything.

About the Author

Christina Neuwirth is a writer and researcher based in Edinburgh. Her short fiction has been published in Gutter and 404 Ink, and her non-fiction can be found in CommonSpace, The Dangerous Women Project, Marbles Mag, and most recently in Nasty Women (404 Ink, 2017) and The Skinny.

She is one of Queer Words Project Scotland's five 2018 Emerging Writers. Christina is currently working on a novel and pursuing a PhD at the University of Stirling, University of Glasgow and Scottish Book Trust, researching gender equality in writing and publishing in Scotland.

Amphibian is her first solo publication.

www.christinaneuwirth.com
@ChristinaNwrth